AGNES PARKER...

Keeping Cool in Middle School

AGNES PARKER...
Keeping Cool in Middle School

By Kathleen O'Dell

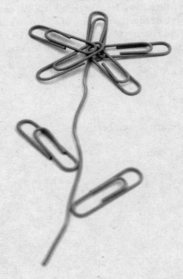

SCHOLASTIC INC.
New York Toronto London Auckland Sydney
Mexico City New Delhi Hong Kong Buenos Aires

ISBN-13: 978-0-545-12908-4
ISBN-10: 0-545-12908-7

12 11 10 9 8 7 6 5 4 3 2 1   9 10 11 12 13/0

Printed in the U.S.A.   40

First Scholastic printing, November 2008

Designed by Teresa Dikun

Text set in Berkely

For Gleeson,
with love . . .

AGNES PARKER...

Keeping Cool in Middle School

CHAPTER ONE

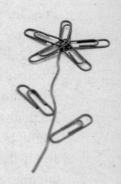

In the far corner of the Horace Mann Middle School locker room, Agnes Parker and her friend Prejean Duval are changing into their gym clothes and keeping their voices low.

"Know what I miss about sixth grade?" Agnes says.

"I give up."

"Gym," Agnes says.

"Huh?" says Prejean. "You've always hated gym."

"Yeah. But last year we got to keep our clothes on!"

Prejean chuckles. "Are you still thinking about Armpit Girl?"

Agnes nods. Yesterday, a girl named Lydia made the mistake of showing up for gym with hairy underarms. Some of the other girls started chanting, "CHEWBACCA!" and Lydia left the locker room in tears.

"Did you know that she dropped out of class?" says Prejean. "She went to the office and had her whole schedule changed."

Agnes finds this perfectly understandable. "Just glad it wasn't me," she says.

Although Agnes knows now that it's important to keep absolutely hairless, she wonders how else she might be out of the loop. Is there something weird about flowered underwear? Or what about these odd tan lines she still has from her summer cutoffs? Will she be called out next?

Fortunately, Peggy Neidermeyer and Carmella Shade are creating a diversion this afternoon. At Agnes's school last year, both girls were rambunctious bullies. Today, they have spent their break tattooing each other's arms with felt pen. Now they're jumping around in their underwear, snapping each other with T-shirts.

"Oh, brother," says a blond girl standing next to Prejean. "Who are the geeks? Could they get any more obnoxious?"

"They went to Woodlands last year," Prejean says. "With us."

"But they're not our friends or anything," Agnes adds quickly.

"They need to get a clue," says the blonde's spiky-haired friend.

"They don't respond to clues," Prejean says flatly.

Agnes recognizes these two girls from her history class. She has noticed the identical tins of hot cinnamon candy that they snack on during class. They wear matching leather belts and the same kind of shoes too. They're the kind of girls who seem to know all the clues.

"Derry and Valerie, right?" Agnes says. "Um, I'm Agnes. From Mr. Dawson's class? This is my friend Prejean."

"Yep," Derry, the blonde, says without enthusiasm. "We've seen you."

"And now we've seen *you*," Prejean says. "So we're even."

Agnes waits for the girls to say something snarky, but they actually smile approvingly. This is Prejean's way: to say exactly what she thinks no matter who she says it to. How does she get away with it?

"We're from Edison," says Derry. As they all head outside, both girls and Prejean are having a conversation while Agnes hangs back, noting that Valerie and Derry fold the elastic waistband low on their gym shorts.

Horace Mann Middle School combines the students from four elementary schools. On the first day, Agnes was swept through the school doors with the crowd, stunned at how bright, crowded, and loud the place was. Two weeks later, the morning jostle still makes her dizzy.

13

Now, as Agnes runs with confident Prejean around the track, she's thinking that maybe her own personality could be perfect for middle school. After all, she's always had a built-in "invisibility factor." Here at Horace Mann, it's as welcome as camouflage, or a force field.

"Did you see the eighth-grade boys," asks Prejean, jogging gracefully, "at the top of the stairwell last period?"

"You mean the boys who were rating all the girls from one to ten?" says Agnes, huffing.

"Not all the girls. The only ones they pick on are seventh graders," Prejean says. "I can't believe teachers let them get away with it."

Agnes is glad that none of them picked on her. She was careful to walk close to the wall and hug her books in front of her chest. *Poof!* The invisibility factor to the rescue.

"I'm just going to ignore all that stuff," Agnes says. "I figure I can keep everything under control if I don't freak out and just concentrate on making it from one class to another. And, also, as long as I have art for homeroom . . ."

"And the incredible, famed Ms. Fabulous-Felson-Morales," finishes Prejean.

"Yes!" says Agnes. "My dream teacher."

Last spring, Agnes's teacher, Mrs. Libonati, wrote a special recommendation to Ms. Felson-Morales suggesting that Agnes would be the perfect student for her art class. After all, Agnes is artistic and Ms. Felson-Morales is an artist, herself. She's also inspirational, fun, and known for having students who turn out astonishing projects. In fact, she was honored as a teacher of the year in Washington, D.C.

The fact that Agnes has her both for art and homeroom seems too good to be true. It makes all the other not-so-good stuff pale in comparison.

"I'm jealous," says Prejean. "My homeroom is a zoo. I don't think I have even one class that makes me excited. Sometimes I look at you, and I think, 'Prejean, don't you wish you were like Agnes? She has *interests*.'"

"I only wish that I could have art all day," Agnes answers. She decides not to tell Prejean how she almost took an after-school job as art room manager. The idea of hanging out in that wonderful classroom, acting as Ms. Felson-Morales's assistant, was tempting. But who would she go home with? Agnes decided to stick close to Prejean.

Just as Agnes starts limping, the gym teacher, Mrs. Newton, blows the whistle for the showers. Agnes bends and rests with her hands on her knees. Prejean isn't even winded.

"Hey, Prejean," says Agnes, "this is our last class. Why don't we just wear our gym clothes and change later?"

"Gotcha," says Prejean. "Then we can shower at home."

Agnes smiles. She and Prejean, best friends since second grade, still know each other inside and out.

Unlike Woodlands Elementary, Horace Mann is too far away for Agnes and Prejean to walk to. Agnes's mom takes the girls to school on her way to work, and Prejean's mom is the picker-upper.

What's strange about today is that Prejean's mom is late. Prejean's mom is never late for anything. Agnes and Prejean sit on the grass, watching all the other kids pile into cars. The two are still sitting there twenty minutes after the crowd has thinned.

"You girls going out for track?"

It's Mrs. Newton calling to them through the chain-link fence.

"We're just waiting for a ride," says Agnes.

"Why are you suited up, then?" Mrs. Newton asks.

"Because Agnes hates showering," Prejean says. Agnes gives Prejean a shove.

"You really oughtta consider trying out," says Mrs. Newton. "You're a natural."

Agnes points to herself. "Me?" she says.

"No!" Mrs. Newton stops herself, then smiles. "I mean, you can try out too, if you want. But I was talking to your friend . . ."

16

Prejean's Honda pulls up to the curb.

"I'll think about it," says Prejean. "But I have to go. This is my mom here."

"Ask her!" says Mrs. Newton. "The team runs for an hour or so after school. We'd love to have you."

"Are you going to do it?" Agnes asks as they fling their backpacks into the trunk.

"I dunno," says Prejean. "I never thought about running before. As a sport. It's just something you do to get from one place to another."

"Still, you're a natural." Agnes puts her hand to her head like a psychic. "Prejean, dahling, I believe you found your *interest*."

"You think so?" Prejean smiles, then opens the car door. "Hey, Mom!" she says. "Why so late?"

Agnes slides into the backseat just in time to see Prejean's expression change.

"Mom?" Prejean asks. "Are you okay?"

"I'm fine, Prejean," says Mrs. Duval in her elegant Jamaican accent.

Prejean squints. "You don't look fine."

"I'm *excellent*, Prejean," says Mrs. Duval. "I've spent all afternoon with the sprinkler repairman, who was doing the job your father was supposed to do last week-end. A tiny little valve is all it needed, which is what I told Claud. You remember, Prejean? But he wouldn't do it, and the thing blew this morning and now I'm out

17

over one hundred dollars . . ."

"But dad was fishing," Prejean says.

"Fishing!" repeats Mrs. Duval. "Suppose I were to go fishing. I'd leave and the whole house would fall apart." She shakes her head. "That man!" she says under her breath.

Prejean doesn't say anything about trying out for track, or how her day went. Mrs. Duval doesn't ask. Agnes waits for the regular conversation to start, but nobody talks until they pull up into Agnes's driveway.

"Thanks, Mrs. Duval," Agnes says.

"You're welcome," she answers, sounding formal.

Prejean holds her pinky finger to her mouth—their sign for "call you later."

Whatever's going on, Agnes will cheer Prejean up later, just like Prejean has done for Agnes a million times. It's all a routine part of the best-friend job, Agnes thinks—and one thing, at least, that they're *both* pretty good at.

CHAPTER TWO

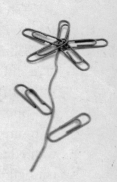

Agnes's mom bangs on the bathroom door. "Agnes, honey, everything okay in there?"

"I'm fine!" says Agnes.

Actually, Agnes was okay until Mrs. Parker knocked and startled her. Now she is soapy, wet, and hopping around, grabbing at toilet paper for her bleeding knee.

"What was that shriek about?" asks Mrs. Parker.

Agnes wraps a towel around herself and opens the door a crack. "Nothing," she says. "I just cut myself shaving."

"Shaving?" asks Mrs. Parker. "Again?"

"Yes," says Agnes, wishing she could just shut the door.

"Oh, you're not using Dad's razor are you? The reason I ask is that he hates it when other people use his razor—"

"Didn't you want something?" Agnes interrupts.

"Oh my goodness," says Mrs. Parker. "Yes. I almost forgot. Prejean's on the phone."

"Could you tell her I'll call her back?" Agnes asks. "I'm still soapy." Agnes closes the door and leans against it. Hadn't she spent over an hour doing homework by the phone? She'd even carried the phone from room to room. And now it's after nine o'clock and all Agnes wanted to do was sneak off and take care of her incriminating knees in private.

As it turns out, the cut is deeper than Agnes first thought. Rinsing off in the shower just makes it worse. Finally, she puts on Neosporin and finds the most giant Band-Aid in the box. No sooner does she get out in the hall than she meets her dad.

Mr. Parker looks down at Agnes's knee, pushes up his glasses, and asks, "Did you fall down today?"

"Something like that," says Agnes as she scoots by. She wastes no time hopping up the stairs to her own bedroom. She flounces on the bed and looks up at the ceiling. *Ahhh!* "Free!" she whispers.

The lamp is still on when the morning alarm goes off. Agnes slips on her glasses and gazes in the mirror. Her hair has dried into crazy tentacles. "I've got to get to work," she says.

Agnes has never been into hair, but she knows that

her invisibility factor depends on looking neither too dorky nor too fluffy. In the meantime, she'll just observe all the kids who look like they know what they're doing until she figures out what the rules are.

It isn't until Mrs. Parker's car approaches Prejean's street that Agnes whaps herself on the forehead. "I didn't call her back," she says to herself.

When Prejean gets into the car, Agnes wails, "I know! I'm sorry!"

"Well, I did call kind of late," says Prejean. "So you're excused."

"That's very nice of you, Prejean," says Mrs. Parker. "By the way, how's your mom?"

"Good-ish, I guess."

"I haven't seen her in a while with this new car pool thing," says Mrs. Parker.

"Yeah, well, that's what I wanted to talk to Agnes about," Prejean says. "I'm going to join track."

"That's great!" Agnes says.

"Sort of. You see, I'm going to be running after school every day and my mom will be picking me up about an hour and a half later."

"Well, Agnes," Mrs. Parker says, "then you'll have to take the metro bus home after school."

"Oh, yeah," says Agnes. The metro bus is crowded with rowdy eighth-grade boys and makes a lot of stops. Sometimes it's so packed, kids have to wait half an hour for a second bus to come by. "That's okay, though," Agnes says, trying to sound casual. "Don't worry."

Prejean gives her an "I'm sorry" look.

"Actually, there is a thing I can do," Agnes says. "Ms. Felson-Morales needs someone four days a week to be in charge of the art room. You know, for cleaning up and stuff. On Wednesdays, I can just wait for you."

"Or," says Mrs. Parker, "you could take the bus. Lots of people do."

"Maybe," says Agnes, although she's already made up her mind that she'd really rather not.

After Mrs. Parker drops them off, Prejean pulls Agnes to her side as they walk down the hallway. "I know you don't want to take that bus. It's just that . . ."

"What?"

"It's just that I really hate hanging around at home lately. My mother is driving me insane! She is always in some sort of fit about my dad, and then she complains to me about him, and I can't stand it."

"Maybe she's just going through a phase. Do you think?" Agnes asks.

"I think," says Prejean, "that my mom's the one who should try running around the track. She needs a hobby or something. Besides nagging, that is."

Agnes tries to give Prejean her full attention, but she can't help being distracted by a growing sense of dread. Ahead, lined up against the wall, are the horrible eighth-grade boys. She stops and grabs Prejean's arm. "Let's turn around and go the other way," she says.

"The art room is just around the corner," says Prejean.

"But I want to go to my locker first."

"But your locker is right by the art room."

"I know, I know," Agnes whispers, "but the boys are *right there*."

Prejean lifts her chin. "Well, isn't it our school *too*? C'mon."

Agnes immediately slinks over so that Prejean is on the "boy side" of the hall.

The girls almost make it past when one of the guys bumps up against Prejean in what Agnes's mother would call an "unacceptable" way. "Oops!" he says in a high voice. "'Scuse me!"

"The skinny one is totally hot," says another.

Prejean wheels around. "Who asked you?" she shouts.

Agnes winces. "I wouldn't yell at them if I were you."

"Why not?" asks Prejean.

"Because they're *eighth-grade boys*."

"Oh, so what?" says Prejean, even more irritated. "And why are we always *whispering*?"

"Shhhhh," says Agnes. "Because we want to stay under their radar, that's why. Otherwise we'll never be able to walk anywhere around here in peace."

Prejean opens her mouth as if to speak, then stops when she notices the hall clock. "Uh-oh," she says.

Agnes looks too. "Shoot. Now I'm not going to have time to go to my locker!" she says.

Prejean blows a movie star kiss. "We'll talk at lunch, dahling!"

It's with some relief that Agnes lugs her books into Ms. Felson-Morales's class. She takes her seat in the wide-open art room, sets down her load of stuff, and gazes up at the rows of windows. Students' mobiles—ingenious structures made of everything from scrap metal to papier-mâché—swirl lazily from the high ceilings like gorgeous satellites. One wall of the classroom is packed with art books, oversized with big glossy pages. The cement floor is streaked with dried and dribbled paint from years of kids making beautiful things.

And the smell! Ms. Felson-Morales has her own little coffee bar behind her desk, giving homeroom a cozy good-morning feel.

"Hello there, people," she says. "Are you ready to do your research?" She holds in her arms a pile of cardboard-mounted photographs. "These are examples of the Cornell boxes we'll be building. After you've looked carefully at each picture, pass it on. Make notes if you like!"

The boy sitting next to Agnes taps her arm. "Hello," he says.

Agnes turns to him and can't help noticing how tiny this kid is. He could pass as a fourth grader, if not for his deep voice and brooding, dark-eyed gaze.

"Hello," says Agnes.

"I am sitting by you today," he says.

"All right," says Agnes.

He keeps staring. Agnes can't think of anything else to say, so she returns her attention to Ms. Felson-Morales.

The boy taps Agnes again and points to her big pile of books. "I see you're skipping the locker thing too," he says.

"I'm not skipping it," says Agnes. "I just didn't have time this morning."

"They stuff you in," he says. "They stuffed my brother in his locker when he was a seventh grader."

"How awful," Agnes says. "Really?"

"It's true. In my family, the boys stay small until they turn fourteen. And then they grow. Big."

"So your brother's big now?" Agnes says.

"Big like the Incredible Hulk. I do not exaggerate."

"Is he green too?" Agnes asks.

"Don't joke," says the boy. "Here is a true story. It is my brother's fourteenth birthday. As soon as he blows out the candles on the cake, his arm muscles puff up and the clothes on his back rip and his Adidas come apart. My mother starts screaming, 'Aram! Aram! Run! Go get a tablecloth!'"

"Why the tablecloth?" asks Agnes.

"Because he was naked and a towel was too small," says the boy. "My aunt and uncle were so embarrassed."

Agnes keeps waiting for the boy to smile or laugh at his own joke, but his gloomy expression never changes.

"So I am waiting for my fourteenth birthday cake. First cake, then locker. Then . . ." Here the boy lifts one black eyebrow.

"What?" asks Agnes.

"Revenge," he says.

Agnes makes a note to keep on the kid's good side. "I'm Agnes," she says. "From Woodlands Elementary."

"I'm Aram Keshishian," he says, "from Oakview."

"Aram and Agnes," says Ms. Felson-Morales as she hands them both photographs. "My *A* students."

"Good one," says Aram. "I will remember you said this at grade time."

Agnes's photo shows a box filled with little stoppered bottles on shelves. Each bottle holds something different: butterfly wings, tiny shells, typed strips of paper, golden powder.

"Joseph Cornell wasn't trained as an artist," says Ms. Felson-Morales. "But he could create worlds out of bits and pieces of throwaway things. Your boxes should

26

hold anything you find personally beautiful or interesting. This is an exercise in staying open to possibilities. Don't be afraid to look for objects in unexpected places."

"Like the garbage?" asks Brian Olansky.

"Sure," says Mrs. Felson-Morales. "But only if the garbage in question is, to you, interesting or beautiful."

Brian pretends to take notes. "Interesting and beautiful garbage," he says.

Agnes sighs heavily. She still can't get over the fact that Brian is in this class. He's the least artsy of any kid she knows. He probably thought the class would be easy.

"Who's this guy?" Aram asks.

"He's a clown," says Agnes. "From my old school."

"You watch," says Aram. "A kid like that? He's going to get stuffed."

"Aram," says Agnes, "are you always the Voice of Doom?"

Aram leans back and presses his fingertips together. "Not always, Miss A. For instance: You, I predict, will *never* get stuffed."

"Because they don't stuff girls," says Agnes.

"Yes," says Aram, "but also because you keep yourself low, minding your business." Aram ducks his head into his neck and looks around furtively.

27

"Is that supposed to be an imitation of me?"

"It's good, isn't it? I've been watching."

"I don't look that bad," Agnes says. "You're kidding me, aren't you?"

"No," says Aram. "That's how you look. Anyway, you don't have to worry. To stuff you would be like stuffing your mother. No one would even try it."

"Well, um, thanks," says Agnes.

"We speak Armenian at home," says Aram with a shrug. "You can tell that English is not my first language."

"I can tell, a little," Agnes says.

Aram leans forward. "Maybe you will think it's part of my charm."

"Mr. A," she says, "please! No more. Your charm is already overpowering."

Agnes, in her own imitation of Aram, gloomily stares him down. Aram stares back. Both of them refuse to smile until Agnes feels her mouth trembling at the corners.

"Not bad for a beginner," says Aram gravely. "I will sit by you again on Monday."

"Okay," Agnes says, already wondering what she's gotten herself into. The "invisibility factor," which is supposed to keep her out of the way of the weird, has in this case definitely backfired.

"Also," says Aram, "I want you to know that anytime you want to work on something after school, you can see me. I have keys to all the supplies."

"Why do *you* have keys?"

"Because," says Aram, "I am the art room manager. Extra credit!"

Agnes's jaw drops. "No!"

"Yes!"

"But I was going to ask Ms. Felson-Morales today, after class . . ."

"You are too late." Aram shrugs.

Visions of the bus appear before Agnes's eyes. Standing in the aisles, swaying and stumbling as the eighth graders yell on either side. "Ugh." She drops her head into her hands. Why didn't she just take the job when it was offered?

"You are taking this very hard, I see," says Aram. "Having the keys, this was a dream of yours?"

The way Aram looks at her, soulful and deeply concerned, makes Agnes feel self-conscious. "It . . . it wasn't a *dream* exactly," she says.

"You wait here," he says.

Aram scoots back his chair and approaches Ms. Felson-Morales. Both student and teacher look over at Agnes, whispering, until the teacher smiles and nods. Aram reaches out, shakes her hand, and makes his way back to Agnes.

"Never fear," he says. "It is fixed."

Agnes warms. "Oh, Aram! You gave up the job? For me?"

"Nooo," says Aram. "This is other good news. You are my assistant. Assistant to the art room manager. I'll make you a name tag, even. How's that?"

"Oh," Agnes says. "Not necessary."

"No problem." He gives her the thumbs-up.

It's better than the bus, Agnes thinks.

Isn't it?

CHAPTER THREE

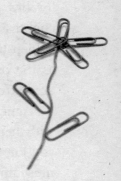

Agnes is grateful for Saturday. Weekends are like little islands where she can hang out, relax, and take everything for granted. She likes it that way.

Today, she plans to gather the makings of a perfect Cornell box. She already has a fixed idea of what she wants. Rather than scouting around for found objects, Agnes is going to create a miniature garden fit for a dollhouse, with paper grass, rows of tiny flowers blooming on green toothpicks, and little birds mounted on springs, flitting in a paper sky.

"I can take you to the hardware store," Mrs. Parker says, "but you'll have to come with me to the grocery store afterward."

"Deal," says Agnes.

She's already found the door she wants for the box's front. It's an old carved wooden picture frame her mom got from a yard sale and never used—the perfect cover for her garden paradise. At the hardware store, she chooses lightweight plywood for the box and some golden hinges. Her mom also lets her buy a little saw, as the one they have back home is sized for cutting down trees.

Agnes, hummingly happy with her art things, chats with her mom on the way to the grocery store. "Do you know that you aren't supposed to take photos in a museum?"

"Mmm-hmm," says Mrs. Parker.

"Ms. Felson-Morales saw a whole bunch of the real Cornell boxes in Paris, and she asked the head guy there to let her take pictures for her class after the museum closed and he said okay."

"Very enterprising," says Mrs. Parker.

"Do you know how many countries Ms. Felson-Morales has visited? Not counting the airports?"

"No idea," says Mrs. Parker.

"Seventeen," says Agnes. "And I've never even been over the border to Canada. Sometimes I wonder if I'm ever going to be a fascinating person."

"Agnes," says Mrs. Parker, "you're already a fascinating person!"

"Doesn't count. You say that because you're my mom."

Agnes sits with her chin in her hand, gazing out

the window. That Aram kid from art class is probably from Armenia. Prejean has been to Jamaica to visit her grandmother. Agnes bets that if she took a poll, she would have been to the least amount of countries of anyone she knows.

"You know, Mom," says Agnes, "sometimes I try to figure out if it's just better to be boring."

"Why would you want to be boring?" Mrs. Parker asks.

"Because you sort of have your privacy," Agnes says. "And people don't bug you. You know what I mean?"

"I'm trying," says Mrs. Parker.

"Like you. You're a good mom and you do your mom things and your job and nothing scary ever happens. But then if you're Ms. Felson-Morales and traveling around the world by yourself, you might end up sharing a train compartment with some shaved-head teenagers who hate Americans and you can't sleep all night and you barely escape with your life!"

Mrs. Parker is silent.

"I think I'm more like you, is what I'm saying." Agnes looks at her mom and smiles, but feels that somehow she's said the wrong thing.

In Higley's Market, Agnes's mom hands her the shopping list. "Could you grab a cart and get started for me?" asks Mrs. Parker. "I have to stand in line for a prescription."

33

"Sure," says Agnes. But as soon as she takes the cart, she feels wary. What if someone from Horace Mann is here? Isn't there something weird about a seventh grader shopping by herself for tomato paste?

Agnes lowers her head and starts plucking items from the shelves. When she spots her mother down at the end of the personal products aisle, she freezes.

Standing next to Mrs. Parker, looking at makeup, are Derry Timms and that spiky-haired Valerie from gym class.

Agnes's mom sees her and starts motioning for her to come over.

Backward? Forward? Which way should Agnes go?

"Over here, honey!" calls Mrs. Parker.

Derry looks up. Caught, Agnes reluctantly makes her way toward her mom.

"Look here!" says Mrs. Parker, flashing a package. "Do you like pink?"

Agnes blinks, horrified. It's a Lady's Choice razor.

"I thought this might be a good one," says Mrs. Parker. "You should have your own now . . ."

Both Derry and Valerie are focused on Agnes, but her mother isn't done yet.

"Or how about blue? This one comes with its own sparkly shaving cream! They call it . . ." Mrs. Parker squints at the package. " . . . *The Flirt*." She kicks up a heel. "Ooo la la!" she says.

Derry and Valerie drop their jaws.

Agnes's vision starts to swim. Shaking, she pushes the cart at her mother and trots blindly out of the store.

Of course, the car is locked. Agnes sits hunched on the back bumper. "Why do I act so stupid?" she murmurs. She knows she's always been shy. But last year, she never had this feeling of having to run from one safe place to another.

When her mom finally rumbles over with the groceries, she sits down beside Agnes.

"Well, that's a first," Mrs. Parker says. "I don't think you've ever run away from me before."

Agnes looks at her mother's face and feels terrible. "I wasn't running away from *you*," says Agnes.

"What was that all about, then?"

"I was embarrassed," Agnes whispers. She pops up briefly to survey the parking lot, then drops back down. "These girls from my school were standing right there."

"Oh," says Mrs. Parker, grimacing. "Was it the razor thing?"

"Yes!" says Agnes. "They were staring at me and I was afraid you were going to do some more . . . acting."

"You used to love my acting," says Mrs. Parker.

"I still sort of do," Agnes lies.

Agnes would hug her mom right now if they weren't sitting on the bumper of their car in an open parking lot. But she figures that her mom probably understands. She was in seventh grade once too, after all.

"Can we get out of here now?" Agnes asks after a long silence.

"As soon as I get the groceries in the trunk," says Mrs. Parker.

Agnes looks over her shoulder. "Can I sit in the car while you do it?"

"Be my guest," says Mrs. Parker.

When they get home, Mr. Parker is there to help unload groceries. Agnes bolts from the car with her package of hardware. Then she takes the phone upstairs, lies on her bed, and dials Prejean.

"Whatcha doing?" Agnes asks.

"Nothing," says Prejean. "How was Higley's?"

"Um, how did you know I was at Higley's?"

"Instant messaging," says Prejean. "I'm in my room IM-ing Natalie and Ashley—you know, just some girls from Woodland Elementary. And then Derry Timms came on. I guess she's sort of friends with Ashley now."

Agnes grits her teeth. "Okay. What did she say?"

"She said something about your mom dancing in the store." Prejean giggles. "I'm like, I know Mrs. Parker. You must have the wrong lady."

"She wasn't dancing! She was . . . I don't know what it was." Agnes feels suddenly protective. "If they're going to say bad stuff, I'd rather they just say it about me."

Prejean is silent.

"Did they say something about me?"

"They say that you shoved a grocery cart at her and ran away."

"Like I was trying to *hurt* her?" Agnes wails. "That makes me sound insane!"

"I told them they must have it wrong. Nat said so too. We all said what a nice normal person you are."

This does not make Agnes feel better.

"Agnes?"

"What?"

"Why don't you just go online with us and make a joke about it? That's what I would do."

"You mean like, 'Hey! Just tried to assassinate my mother with a grocery cart! Boy, are we *both* crazy!'"

"Oh come on," Prejean says. "I'll help."

Agnes hangs up and runs downstairs to the den. The laptop is missing from its place on the desk. She makes her way toward the kitchen, where her mom and dad are putting away the groceries, and stops when she hears her name. Carefully, she tiptoes around the corner and holds her breath.

"But Rosemary," says Agnes's dad, "remember how well she did at summer camp? You were worried about that too."

"I know," says Mrs. Parker. "It was great to see her

do so well. Especially after being in a cabin where she didn't know a soul. I just thought that all that new confidence would translate to middle school."

Agnes is stunned. She replays what she's just heard and tries to figure out what it means.

"Give it time," says Mr. Parker. "This isn't necessarily a step backward. She's never been very outgoing. It's natural that she's going to be a little nervous."

"I wish you could see *how* nervous," says Mrs. Parker. "I'm concerned."

Agnes finally takes a breath. Her eyes are stinging. She feels like she has just taken a blow.

As she stumbles away, she catches sight of the laptop on the entryway table.

She doesn't dare pick it up. There are people on the computer. Talking, talking, talking!

"Is there one place I can go in this entire universe where people aren't discussing how weird I am?" she asks the mirror.

Agnes climbs upstairs, lies on her bed staring at the ceiling, and stays there, motionless.

Maybe her mother is right. Maybe she *is* going backward.

"All right, Agnes Parker," she tells herself. "Get a grip. "

She turns over onto her stomach, rests her head in her hands, and frowns, vowing not to leave the house until she figures out who she's going to be on Monday.

CHAPTER FOUR

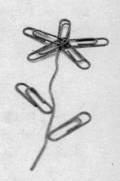

The Agnes who comes to school on Monday is determined not to resemble the freaked-out friend Prejean spoke to on Saturday. But Prejean is too fired up with her own stuff to notice. She sits in the lunchroom with Agnes, Ashley, and Natalie, ignoring her pizza, talking a mile a minute.

"Now for the good part!" Prejean says, leaning in close. "Listen. I've got a huge favor to ask you."

"Such as?" Agnes says.

"I want to run for class president."

"Yay!" says Natalie.

"And I want Agnes to be my campaign manager." Prejean grins and thumps both hands flat on the table.

Agnes jumps. "When did you decide all this?" she asks.

"Yesterday," says Prejean.

"We were all talking about it online," says Ashley.

Prejean cocks her head. "By the way, where were you all weekend?"

"Working on a project," Agnes says. *Me*, she thinks.

"Anyway," continues Prejean, "I'm claustrophobic. I spent the entire weekend hiding from my parents. They are not getting along and there is nothing I can do. And so, when some of us were talking about the things that bug us here, I decided. I am going to do something. Why? Because I can."

"Aren't you supposed to fill out some papers or something?" Agnes asks. "What's the deadline?"

"Today," says Prejean. "I already have my platform. STUPID EIGHTH-GRADE BOYS—LAY OFF GIRLS IN THE HALLS."

Agnes wants to shout, *Are you crazy?* But all she says is, "Sort of sudden, don't you think?"

"*Life* is sudden," says Prejean.

"Not *my* life," Agnes says.

"Oh, come on!" Prejean says.

"I'm considering it," Agnes says, trying to sound un-freakoutable.

Prejean lowers her chin. "You aren't the one running for president. All you have to do is put in some time after school and make the buttons and maybe pass them out in the halls and—"

"Pass them out in the halls?"

40

Prejean slaps the table again. "Agnes Parker, honestly! I can't believe you won't help me. All I'm asking is . . ."

Agnes stops hearing Prejean's words. Coming toward their table are Derry and Valerie. Both are eating identical ice cream bars and wearing the exact same shade of shimmery fingernail polish.

"Ick," Agnes says, closing her eyes.

Prejean looks over her shoulder.

"Hey, PJ," says Derry.

"It's Prejean," says Prejean. "Hi."

"Hi, Agnes," says Valerie.

Agnes feels her shoulders draw up around her ears. Then she remembers Aram's imitation of her and sits up straight. "Hello," she says.

"Wasn't it you we saw at Higley's Market?" asks Derry.

"When?" Agnes asks, straight-faced.

"Saturday," says Valerie, rolling her eyes.

Agnes fakes thinking it over. "Oh, yeah . . . I was there."

Both girls smirk, turn to each other, and mouth the word *psycho*.

Agnes can feel herself perspiring. She clears her throat and tries to smile. "Did you hear that Prejean is going to run for class president?"

"Yay!" shouts Natalie again. "I'm her official cheerleader."

41

"Do you, like, think you're going to win?" asks Valerie.

"Why not?" says Ashley. "You should know that Prejean is *very* cool."

"We all want her to win!" Agnes declares. "That's why I'm going to be her campaign manager."

"You're saying yes, then?" Prejean asks.

"Yes, I am saying yes." Agnes folds her hands. "So, Valerie and Derry—are you going to vote for her?"

Derry and Valerie shrug in unison.

"You really should. She'd be great. The best." Agnes gestures to her friend as if Prejean is the grand prize on *The Price Is Right*.

"Thank you, campaign manager," says Prejean.

"Tell your friends," Agnes says.

Judging from their blank expressions, Derry and Valerie may have already forgotten why they came over to the table. *Distraction accomplished!*

"We'll think about it," says Derry at last. The girls turn and walk in lockstep to another table.

"Thank you!" Agnes calls after them.

"Now that," says Prejean, "was completely random. What's gotten into you?"

"I want to be your campaign manager," Agnes says.

"I got that," says Prejean.

"As long as I don't have to be too much out front," Agnes says.

"You were pretty much out front with those two," Prejean says.

"Was I?" Agnes says, pleased.

"So what should me and Ashley do?" asks Natalie.

"I was thinking you guys could go around to the people we already know from Woodlands."

"I can do even more than that," Natalie says. "A ton of Horace Mann kids go to the Korean Presbyterian church. I've put in nine years of Sunday school with them."

"And I can do more things online," says Ashley.

"I'll do anything," Agnes says, "as long as you don't make me talk into a microphone or yell things to eighth-grade boys. I'm more into sign- and button-making."

"I'll do the yelling, you do the selling," Prejean says.

Agnes bites her thumbnail and thinks. The other kids have their campaigns under way. In fact, the two existing presidential candidates already have big posters in the cafeteria.

THE MAN FOR MANN:
VOTE FOR MATTHEW BLACKER
7TH GRADE PRESIDENT!

and

MCVOTE FOR SHANE MCNEENY!
7TH GRADE CLASS PREZ!

Agnes pulls out a piece of paper and starts doodling.

PREJEAN DUVAL—THAT'S ALL!
PREJEAN 4 PREZ

Hmmm. Could she put that in a four-leaf clover?

Prejean gets up and looks over Agnes's shoulder. "Cute," she says. "Keep thinking. We have a lot of catching up to do."

Agnes doesn't know much about the presidential competition. "Maybe it's a good thing that they're both boys," she says.

"Exactly what I was thinking," Prejean says. "I can go all out for the girl vote on girl issues."

"Have you heard anything about the two guys?"

"Well, Shane's one of the boys who hang out in the hall with the eighth graders. I guess his brother lets him tag along. He's a slacker type, loud. Oh, and Ashley has a *huge* thing for him."

"And that's an exact quote, I'll bet," says Agnes. The joke about Ashley is that she always has a "huge thing" going for many boys at a time.

"The other guy I heard comes from Oakview," Prejean says.

"The Man for Mann?"

"Isn't that dumb?" says Prejean. "But from what I hear, he's the real competition. He's a genius jock

44

type of guy who's probably going to win."

"Except now, he has the *Woman* for Mann on his tail," Agnes laughs.

Prejean makes a muscleman pose. "Me!" she says in a caveman voice. "Woman for Mann!"

"Ooo! How about this one?" breathes Agnes. "Prejean Duval: Because a *Mann* needs a *Woman*."

"Now you're scaring me," says Prejean.

"Hey, you're the one who hired me for my creative whatever," says Agnes.

In gym, thanks to Derry and Valerie, several girls come up to Prejean to talk about her campaign.

"The big reason I'm running," she tells them, "is because I think that we shouldn't have to be embarrassed by eighth-grade boys every time we walk down the halls."

"I've wondered about that too," says Pat Marie, a plump, shy girl from Agnes's old school. "I know some girls already complained."

"I'll tell you how they get away with it," says Derry. "They just move their little group around. When they get kicked out of the stairwell, they stand in front of the library. When they get kicked out of there, they stand by the cafeteria."

"So it sounds like you'll be voting for Prejean," says Agnes.

"I don't know," says Derry.

"Why not?" asks Pat Marie.

"Because boys are like that," says Derry. "It's not going to help to get all mad at them."

"Boys don't like naggy girls," says Valerie, arranging her hair. "It's called teasing. Either ignore it or take it as a joke."

Agnes is watching to see how Prejean will respond, when bully Peggy Neidermeyer bellows from across the room.

"Aw, who gives a rat's banana about what the boys think?"

The conversation stops dead.

"We do!" Derry finally hollers back.

"Some of us," says Valerie pointedly, "still like *boys*."

Neidermeyer's buddy Carmella says, "Whoa!" Neidermeyer throws her tennis shoes to the floor and stomps over.

Valerie crosses her arms over her chest. "Oh no! She's not going to try to wrestle with us, is she?"

"I wouldn't waste my time," says Neidermeyer, squinching up an eye.

"Me neither," chimes in Carmella.

"I'm with Prejean," declares Neidermeyer, "and her little friend Geeky."

Agnes and Prejean give each other shocked looks.

"Geeky!" echoes Carmella.

"They call her *Geeky*?" Valerie whispers to Derry.

"It's our widdle pet name for her," Neidermeyer baby-talks.

"Thanks a lot," grumbles Agnes.

"Prejean," says Derry, suddenly sincere, "you seem like a nice person. But if the misfits are your people? You're not off to a great start."

Agnes can tell by the flare of Prejean's nostrils that her friend is about to say something that, candidate-wise, she might regret. She places her hand on Prejean's shoulder. "How about we run now, okay?" Agnes gently suggests.

"Okay," says Prejean through gritted teeth.

Prejean runs all through gym class and keeps on running for an entire hour after school. Agnes doesn't start her art room job until next week, so she sits on the bleachers outside, sketching ideas and slogans for Prejean's campaign.

Every once in a while she gazes at Prejean—her bobbing ponytail and her untiring runner's stride. She looks magnificent, actually. Heroic. Who wouldn't vote for her?

Then she gets an excellent idea:

PREJEAN DUVAL, Agnes writes. RUNNING FOR CHANGE.

"That's it," she says to herself. It tells the whole story, without being too corny.

All she needs now is to get a picture of Prejean running around the track, scan it through her computer, blur the image, and tint it charcoal and white—something to make it more punchy and graphic. And what about trailing her black-lettered slogan behind in a streak of red—Horace Mann's school colors?

The next evening Agnes runs her designs by her father, who's a graphic artist.

"Agnes, these look really good," he says. "Wow."

Agnes beams. Her father is a quiet, dreamy, keep-to-himself type. He doesn't say "wow" too often.

"I think you've done a great job all by yourself. The only thing is, you're going to need larger images than our home computer can give you," he says.

"I was thinking that too," Agnes says.

"Can I take these into work? I could blow this up for you."

"I thought you'd never ask," Agnes says. "And could you make copies too?"

"Anything for the cause," Mr. Parker says. He scratches his chin. "Has your mother seen these?"

"Not yet."

"Let's show her," he says.

Agnes waits while her dad calls, "Rosemary!" Mrs. Parker peeks her head in the den, then spots the posters and raises her eyebrows.

"Did your dad do these?" she asks.

"Nope. Me," Agnes answers.

"Agnes, these are amazing," declares Mrs. Parker. She drapes her arm around her daughter and squeezes.

"Thank you very much," Agnes says, glowing.

Agnes takes her work upstairs so she can spread everything out on her bed and daydream. She thinks about the poster of Prejean, the runner, out front and going the distance. How often has she wished she could trade Prejean's "outie" personality for her own "innie"?

Tonight, Agnes shrugs off the thought. Instead she anticipates the look on her friend's face when she sees this poster on the wall. Prejean Duval, outie, is going to be blown away!

CHAPTER FIVE

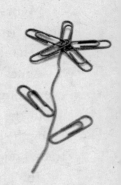

Agnes puts in several days of after-school work just to get the posters assembled. Every day Aram is in the art room, cleaning brushes, putting away supplies.

"I'm not much of an assistant, am I, Aram?"

"So far?" Aram says. "Grade D."

"Sorry. At least I clean up my own mess."

"Do you see the posters in the cafeteria?" Aram asks. "The paint is drippy! Matthew and Shane finished theirs last week in one lunch hour. They're the ones who left all the lids off our tempera."

"Prejean is getting nervous," Agnes says. "But I told her that if I went faster, her signs would look as sloppy as everybody else's."

Unlike Prejean's competitors, Agnes refuses to muck up her beautiful work with ugly taped corners. She has brought her own poster-mounting gum. The giant lettering for each sign has been computer-printed, cut out by hand, and carefully glued. But it's the black-and-white photo of Prejean streaking down the track that gives the sign its punch.

When Prejean joins Agnes in the cafeteria to hang the first poster, all her doubts are silenced.

"Agnes, I swear," says Prejean, catching her breath, "I'm seriously awestruck." She backs up and studies the poster again. "You could put this on a billboard. It's like real advertising."

"I have to admit," Agnes declares, "it makes the guys' signs look a little like grade-school stuff."

Agnes hangs another sign in the main hallway and another by the girls' bathroom. By the next morning, everyone knows who Prejean Duval is.

When Agnes enters homeroom, two people who never spoke to her before come over to introduce themselves.

"Isn't that your friend running for president?" one girl asks.

"Yes, and you have to promise to vote for her," says Agnes.

"I'll vote for her!" volunteers Brian Olansky.

"Tell everybody, Brian," Agnes says.

Ms. Felson-Morales looks up from her desk. "Those posters are gorgeous, Agnes. You put the time in and it shows."

Agnes can feel herself blush.

"Not only are the graphics exceptional," continues Ms. Felson-Morales, "but you get extra points for your political involvement." She smiles warmly. "Brava."

"I clean all the messes, you get all the teacher-love," says Aram. "Where do I complain?"

"Alas, life is not fair, Mr. A," says Agnes, wiping away an imaginary tear. But inwardly, she feels terrific.

At lunch, Natalie and Ashley join Prejean and Agnes in cutting out buttons. All four girls snip with scissors until their hands cramp.

"Prejean," says Natalie, "I'll help any way you want. But now I gotta have some lunch. The smell of grilled cheese is actually making me drool."

"My hands are claws," moans Ashley, inspecting her shimmery fingernail polish.

"Go take a break," says Prejean, "and thank you, guys. You're the best."

Agnes makes room for Natalie and Ashley to get up. "Are you going to grab a sandwich too, Prejean?"

"Nope."

"Did you bring your own?"

"Nope."

"You wanna share mine?" Agnes asks.

"Actually, I'm not hungry," says Prejean. "I'm going to keep working."

"You've got some strong hands," Agnes says.

"The least I can do is help out at lunch. I'd pitch in after school too, but I gotta do my running."

Agnes opens a pack of raisins and sighs. She can't believe how much work there still is to be done. Each button must now be colored in with a red swoosh. It's going to take hours and hours . . .

"Hello, Miss A. You are very busy, I see." Aram is standing with one shoulder weighted down by an enormous backpack.

"Mr. A," says Agnes. "What a surprise."

"Mr. A!" says Prejean. "I've heard so much about you."

"And I've *seen* all about you on the walls," says Aram.

"Oh Aram." Agnes winces. "Would you please put that backpack down? It hurts me just looking at you."

"I am building muscle," Aram says proudly.

"So are we," says Prejean, flexing and unflexing her hand. "Cutting and coloring muscles."

"You need help with this?" asks Aram.

"Yes!" Agnes says. "I'll be bringing this stuff to the art room later."

"Put the boy to work," commands Prejean.

"I could have helped you today, if you asked me." He lowers his voice. "You will need a lot of help to beat Matthew Blacker."

"Why do you say that?" Prejean asks.

"He was king at my old school, you know? I'm try-ing to think of how to say it . . ." Aram rubs his chin. "He isn't bad or mean. But it is like he is made out of machine parts."

"I don't get it," Prejean says.

"I mean he does everything perfectly." Aram straightens his arms and cocks his head robotically. "See?"

Prejean laughs. "Yes! I get it now."

"We have to remove his microchip while he's sleep-ing," whispers Agnes.

"Now that is a plan," says Aram. "After school we'll talk about it, right? In our classroom. You know where."

"Gotcha," says Agnes.

As soon as he's out of earshot, Prejean sings, "You've got a fan, Agnes!"

"He's not my fan," Agnes states. "He's a friend. Kind of. Also, he's got a thing against the eighth-grade boys too. He likes your message, that's all."

"Uh-huh," Prejean says slyly.

That afternoon, Aram makes the time fly by telling impossible stories. Like the one about his chess-master great-grandfather who carved game pieces out of Persian cucumbers as a centerpiece for his son's wedding ban-quet. Or the aunt who discovered that her soup always tastes better when she cooks blindfolded.

"Oh, that's nothing," Agnes tells him. "My father does everything blindfolded. He even drives that way."

"I can't believe you," Aram says.

"And my mother? She's just out of her mind. An insane person. When my father goes out driving blindfolded, he takes her along in the trunk of the car." Agnes gives Aram a stony stare. "How'm I doing?" she asks.

"Better," Aram says.

By the end of the week, between lunch and the art room, they have four hundred buttons cut, colored, and pinned.

"Aram, you must think I'm a slave driver. I'll bet you can hardly wait to get back to your old friends."

"My 'old friends' is one friend. He is also my cousin. Edwin Vartinian. I can wait."

"You sound like you're not too crazy about him."

"*Crazy* would not be the word. I am like his brother. We know what the other person is going to say. We come from the same kind of families. I don't have to explain, but then I can't surprise him."

"You're always surprising me," Agnes says.

"You're easy," Aram says.

"You'll be glad to know we're almost done. All we have to do is pass these out in the halls," says Agnes.

"I can't help with that," says Aram. "Sorry."

"Too 'out there' for you?"

Aram nods. "If I were fourteen, I could do it. You know I would."

Agnes leans her cheek on her hand and yawns. "I do," she says.

"I like your glasses," says Aram. "They are very thick and make your eyes look small."

"Terrific," says Agnes.

"Like tiny sapphires," he emphasizes. "I like seeing them after school."

"Well, I'll still be bringing them along with me Monday to homeroom, so you won't have to miss them that much."

As Agnes packs up her colored pencils, she realizes that she has started looking forward to seeing Aram. With him, she never has to watch her step. There's something remarkably freeing about having a boy type of friend you can say absolutely anything to. Especially here at Horace Mann.

When Agnes awakes on Saturday morning, her brain is foggy. The sunshine on the wall is extraordinarily bright. She checks her alarm clock and sits upright.

"It's one o'clock!"

She's been sleeping later on weekends, but never this late. Downstairs she finds her mom and dad eating lunch at the kitchen table.

"Mom!" she says. "How come you didn't wake me up?"

"I almost did," says Mrs. Parker. "But then I thought you might need the rest."

Agnes sits and steals a chunk of cantaloupe from her father's plate. "Whoo. I've been working hard, but not that hard."

"I know," says Mrs. Parker. "But your dad and I were talking this morning, and we think you're going through a growth spurt. Like Prejean last spring."

"Finally," says Agnes.

"It makes you sleepy," says Mr. Parker. "From what I remember."

Agnes grabs a pencil from the cup by the phone. "Let's measure and see."

She backs up against the doorway where her mom has been marking her height since second grade.

"Heels against the wall," says her mom. "Are you sure you aren't cheating?"

"How can you cheat at height?" Agnes asks. She turns to look at her new mark.

"I believe you've grown about one and a half inches," says her mother.

"Since July?" Agnes looks down to the September of sixth grade. "Ohmigosh. Look at what a shrimp I was last year."

"You weren't a shrimp," says her mother. "You were adorable."

The doorbell rings. Agnes rushes to answer and

skids toward the door in her slipper socks. When she opens the door, there's Prejean in her gym shorts and running shoes.

"Gee, Agnes. Pajamas?" she says.

"Slept in," says Agnes. And then she examines Prejean's face. She doesn't appear to have been crying, but her lips are dry and bitten and there's a deep crease in the middle of her forehead. "What's wrong?"

"My dad," says Prejean.

"Is he okay?" Agnes asks.

"Let's go in the backyard," says Prejean. "I don't want your mom to hear."

Once the girls are seated at the patio table, Prejean announces: "A week ago, my dad said he was going to take some time off and go fishing."

"Not unusual," says Agnes.

"Except for the length of time. Since when does he leave us alone for a week?"

"So what's happening?"

"Dad's not just fishing. He's actually living at the cabin," says Prejean.

"No!" says Agnes.

"I wasn't going to wait forever to find out what's going on. So I followed my mother around for twenty-four hours saying, 'Where's Dad?' And every time, she'd say, 'Fishing.' So then I'd say, 'No, *really*. Where's Dad?' I just told myself I was going to wear her down."

Agnes can completely picture this, considering that Mrs. Duval and Prejean are the two most stubborn people she knows. "When you say twenty-four hours, you don't mean that you bugged her all night, do you?"

"Almost," says Prejean. "I snuck into bed with her at about two in the morning, and as soon as she popped open her eyes I was right there in her face asking, 'Where's Dad?' That's when she gave up and told me he's gone."

"Do you know why he left?"

Prejean hesitates. "It's hard to tell. I know he gets mad when my mom pesters him."

Agnes has seen Mr. Duval grit his teeth on several occasions when Mrs. Duval scolds him for leaving the garage door open or forgetting to bring in the trash cans.

"Anyway," says Prejean, "all my mom will say is that they're taking a break from each other."

"But what does that mean?" asks Agnes. "Could he change his mind and come back?"

"I guess so," says Prejean. "Everything is up in the air." She folds her arms and rests her head on the table. "I hate everything up in the air," she says.

"And why can't my mom find out?" asks Agnes.

"Because my dad could still come back. And I had to pry the truth out of my mom. And . . . I'm embarrassed."

"I understand," Agnes says. She knows that if she were in Prejean's shoes, she'd be embarrassed too. Not because anything was her fault. It's a privacy thing.

"Do you want to walk to Mr. Hahn's store?" Agnes suggests. "I'll buy you some Dubble Bubble and barbecue potato chips."

Prejean lifts her head. "Ugh. I am so not hungry right now."

"Do you want to stay overnight here?" Agnes asks. "We could rent a dumb movie or something."

"No, thanks. I don't want my mom to be alone."

"What can I do, Prejean?"

Prejean puts her forehead back on the table. "Make my dad come back," she says.

"Okay," says Agnes. "Do you have his phone number?"

"Ha," says Prejean, not looking up. "Not funny."

How can Agnes possibly say what she wants to say? That the thought of opening up her own father's closet and seeing that everything is gone—it's enough to bring tears to her eyes.

Agnes's sentences are stuck. Both girls sit wordlessly until Agnes's stomach makes an animal growl.

"Was that you?" Prejean asks.

"Sorry," says Agnes. "It's almost two and I haven't had anything to eat. Want to get a donut?"

Prejean makes a face. "Nah."

"Will you come with me to get a donut, then?"

"I think I'll keep running, if that's all right with you," says Prejean. "It takes my mind off things. And anyway, the smell of a donut shop right now would just make me sick."

"Donut smells are good smells, Prejean," says Agnes.

"Not to me." Prejean stands and stretches. "Lately, food smells are grossing me out. And then when I make myself eat, I get horrible stomachaches."

"That's terrible!" says Agnes. "So that's why you don't eat lunch anymore."

"You noticed, huh?"

Agnes quickly stands up. "Prejean, what did you have for breakfast?"

Prejean sighs. "Cracker," she mumbles.

"Crackers with an 's'?"

"Nope. Just one cracker."

"Lunch?" Agnes asks.

"Water," says Prejean.

"You're kidding."

Prejean stamps her foot. "Don't make a big deal out of this, please. And don't talk to anyone about this. If you knew what it felt like to have my stomach, you wouldn't be eating either."

Agnes circles Prejean's wrist with her thumb and finger. "Look how little you are. You need food! More than even a normal person."

"I *am* a normal person," Prejean growls.

Agnes throws up her hands. "Okay, okay."

"And now, I am going to run."

As her friend lopes away, Agnes can't help but yell after her. "WATER IS NOT A FOOD GROUP!"

But Prejean continues jogging . . . with her fingers in her ears.

Agnes sits by herself for a long time before she goes inside the house. Then, on her way to her room, she stops in the kitchen doorway and watches her mother emptying the dishwasher. *Help!* she thinks. But she can't say anything because keeping a promise is the only truly friend-like thing she can do.

Weekends don't feel like an island anymore. It's Agnes who feels like an island.

CHAPTER SIX

With only one week left until the election, Prejean works the halls before school and during breaks. Most people take a campaign button from her, but Agnes keeps finding them thrown on the floor.

"Try to get them to pin the button on," Agnes suggests.

"I have been," says Prejean. "You know, Matthew Blacker's buttons are stickers. They're easy to put on and they stay put."

"But ours are reusable!" says Agnes, stooping to pick up another dropped button. "Dang. Someone stepped on this one."

"Maybe I'll tape them to people when I do the cafeteria during lunch," Prejean says.

"No, you are going to *eat* during lunch," Agnes says. "Don't worry. I'll get Natalie and Ashley to help out."

At noon, Agnes stations Natalie and Ashley by the cafeteria doors and arms them with buttons and tape. "Tell everyone who takes one that you know Prejean, and that she's the best," says Agnes. "By *far* the best."

"Ahem," says Ashley.

"You might want to turn around, Agnes," says Natalie.

Two boys have parked themselves on the other side of the cafeteria doors. One of the kids wears a paper vest with graffiti scrawled on the back. Stickers cover the front of their shirts:

MATTHEW BLACKER: YOUR MAN FOR MANN! BLACKER BACKER!

"Not fair," says Natalie. "We were here first."

Ashley flashes them a lip-glossy smile. "What's your platform?" she asks.

Both boys hold up a fist. "Blacker's the *man*!" they yell.

"Did you know that Matthew was president at his old school?" Agnes asks Natalie and Ashley.

"He's popular," Ashley says. "The other guy, Shane? He's just in it for fun, I guess."

Agnes can't help but smirk a little. "Hey, Ashley, don't you have a *huge* thing for him?"

Ashley thinks this one over. "Hmm. I wouldn't say *huge*. He's more like one of my, oh, top five?"

"He's in my bio class," says Natalie. "He hasn't brought in any homework yet. He's that kind of guy."

"And he rates the girls too, remember?" says Agnes. "He's like the eighth graders' mascot."

Ashley gives Natalie a nudge. "Oh! I almost forgot. Shane's eighth-grade brother? If you think Shane's cute—and I do—his brother's, like, good-looking to the point of unbelievable."

"So what?" says Natalie. "He's a butthead."

"Which doesn't make him any less good-looking," Ashley insists.

"Out of all the eighth-grade guys, he's the worst," says Natalie. "He is the enemy, Ashley."

Agnes pictures Shane now, with his flip-flops and his shirt halfway unbuttoned, always standing near a guy with blond dreadlocks. "Doesn't his brother have a dog name?"

"Rex," says Natalie.

Suddenly, Ashley frowns. "Hey, Agnes, didn't you say Neidermeyer was voting for Prejean?"

Agnes follows Ashley's gaze and sees Neidermeyer and Carmella approaching the Men for Mann.

"Traitors," Natalie says.

"Got a sticker for me?" booms Neidermeyer, holding out her hand.

"Me too!" says Carmella.

"I got friends," says Neidermeyer. "Better make it two!"

"Make it four!" says Carmella.

Agnes grudgingly notes the boys' smug expressions as both girls gather up fistfuls of Blacker propaganda. "Unbelievable," she murmurs.

But then, before anyone says anything else, Neidermeyer and Carmella sharply tear the stickers in neat little pieces.

"Whoopeee!" says Neidermeyer, tossing the torn paper in the air like confetti. Carmella sprinkles hers over the boys' shoes.

"Sorry!" says Neidermeyer. "We changed our minds."

"That's asking for it," says one of the boys.

"Get down and pick it up," says the other. "*Now*."

"Don't think so," says Neidermeyer. Smiling broadly, the girls skip over to Agnes's side. Neidermeyer salutes. "Two Prejean buttons, please!"

"You are going to wish you'd never done that," vows the boy with the vest.

Natalie and Ashley pin on the buttons, while Agnes says "I'm sorry!" to the guys.

"You *will* be," says one of the boys.

"Don't say you're *sorry*, Aglet," moans Neidermeyer. "Or is Wimpy still your second language?"

"No need to get nasty, Neidermeyer," Ashley says.

"Also, do not offend us," says Neidermeyer stiffly. "We're voters, ya know."

Agnes feels a push from behind. The cafeteria doors are open and a swarm of kids finished with lunch move in for buttons.

Carmella and Neidermeyer walk backward, waving. "No hard feelings, Agnes Parker!" Neidermeyer says.

Agnes considers that this is Neidermeyer being friendly. Maybe it's the best she can do?

She decides to go over to the Blacker backers, who are peeling and sticking buttons to anyone and everyone who passes.

"I just wanted to tell you, that girl is not with Prejean's campaign," she says. "Believe me, we didn't put her up to anything . . ."

The kid in the vest smashes a Blacker sticker in the center of Agnes's forehead. "That's nice," he says.

Trembling, Agnes rips off the sticker. "I'm just trying to apologize."

"Excuse me," says Prejean, striding up. "But what do you think you're doing?"

"Where did you come from?" Agnes asks.

"I saw what you just did," Prejean says, ignoring Agnes. "That was completely rude and out of line."

"If you don't like it," says the boy, "don't have your friends vandalize our campaign materials."

"Agnes," says Prejean, heating up, "would never vandalize anything."

"He's talking about Neidermeyer," Agnes says.

"I don't care who you're talking about," Prejean says. "I don't wanna see you sticking things on my best friend's face again. *Is that clear?*"

Agnes covers her eyes. "Aauuuugh! ENOUGH!" When she drops her hands, Prejean and the boys have shut up.

"You, Prejean, come with me," Agnes says, grabbing her friend by the sleeve. As she drags her toward the girl's bathroom, Agnes sees the notorious gang of eighth-grade boys leaning against the wall up ahead. She stops.

"Prejean," says Agnes, "do you see what I see? The kid in the middle, right next to Rex McNeeny?"

"Shane." Prejean seethes silently for a moment, then declares, "I'm going to talk to him."

"Nuh-nuh no," Agnes says. "You are coming to the bathroom with me."

"It'll only take a second," says Prejean, breaking away.

Agnes hangs back as her friend steamrolls her way toward the boys.

"High seven!" yells one kid.

"Nine!"

"Eight!"

Prejean is almost nose to nose with Shane and has her finger pointed at his chest.

"Three!" he says. And the boys all laugh.

Prejean sets her jaw. "That's flattering coming from a two," she says.

Shane raises his hands holdup style.

"Feisty!" says Rex.

"I just want you to know that there are a lot of girls—*a lot*—who are sick and tired of you guys. And if Shane thinks standing here is going to win him any votes, he's wrong."

"Stop!" says Shane. "You're frightening me!"

"Good," Prejean shouts, "because you don't frighten me." Then she balls up her fist and belts him in the arm, hard.

The boys howl. "Did you just punch me?" says Shane, rubbing his arm in disbelief.

Prejean punches him again—harder! "Does that answer your question?" she says. She turns on her heel and marches back to Agnes, a vein pulsing on her forehead.

Agnes hopes the scene is almost over, but Neidermeyer and Carmella jump in as reinforcements. Neidermeyer windmills her arms, then freezes with her palms open, like a mime.

"In your *face*!" she shouts.

"Your face, your face, your face!" Carmella chants as she hops around like a gnome.

"Anything but *your* face," says Rex.

"Minus eleven!" declares Shane.

By now, a bunch of kids are watching. Huddled by their lockers, Derry and Valerie, looking mortified, are whispering.

What's worse, Agnes knows what they are saying and why they're right. The last thing Prejean's campaign needs at this moment is the Neidermeyer/Carmella endorsement.

"Come with me, Prejean," Agnes says firmly, "and do not stop."

As soon as the girls are behind closed doors, Agnes turns on Prejean. "What do you think you're going to accomplish by going around hitting people? Is that your way of reaching out?"

Prejean folds her arms. "You sound like Derry and Valerie."

"Oh no you don't," says Agnes. "This isn't about me. It's about you. You're acting weird."

Agnes waits for Prejean to argue back, but she stands silent.

"I'm worried about you," Agnes says. Then, softly, "Come on, Prejean. Talk to me."

Prejean slumps and leans against the tile wall. "I'm tired."

"You don't look good," Agnes says. "In fact, I'm tempted to give you a three myself."

Prejean smiles weakly. "I feel like a three."

Agnes wonders what happened to the girl who was running around as if her pants were on fire just moments ago. "Are you eating anything?" she asks.

"I can't," Prejean says. "I try, but every time I do, my stomach hurts. Sometimes I have to lie down."

"Maybe it's time to go to the doctor?"

"But I don't think I have a disease or anything," Prejean says.

"How do you know?"

Prejean blows the bangs from her eyes. "Mostly, I just want to yell at everyone all the time. I wake up mad and for the rest of the day, everything anyone says or does seems stupid."

"Have you heard anything from your dad?"

"No," says Prejean. "He came back yesterday to get some clothes when I was gone. It's like our whole family is balancing on a wire. It's not a friendly house anymore."

The bathroom is starting to fill with girls. Prejean goes into a stall while Agnes waits by the sink. Natalie rushes in and nearly bumps into her.

"Agnes," says Natalie. "I've been looking for you."

"Why? More fighting with the Blacker boys?"

"Ashley's out there doing just the opposite." Natalie wrinkles her nose. "Naturally, she thinks they're cute." She leans in closer to Agnes. "What I want to ask you is, how's Prejean?"

Agnes widens her eyes and points frantically to stall number two. "She's fine! Just fine."

"Oops," Natalie says. She whispers in Agnes's ear, "There's something going on with her. Do you know what it is?"

Agnes quickly shakes her head.

"Really? Huh." Natalie narrows her eyes. "You're sure."

"Absolutely," says Agnes.

"Maybe we can talk later," Natalie whispers. Then, in a stagey voice, she says: "Well, I better get going to class!"

Prejean pokes her head out of the stall as soon as Natalie is gone. "Was she talking about me?"

"She just wants to know if you're okay."

Prejean rolls her eyes. "I hope you said yes."

"Be honest with me," Agnes says. "What did you have for lunch?"

"Don't worry," Prejean says. "I had a roll."

"That's all?"

Prejean nods.

"Prejean!" Agnes says. "And I suppose you're going to run after school too?"

"It gives me energy," Prejean says, irritated. "Running and being mad give me energy. And I'm sorry, but I can't talk about it anymore."

Agnes knows Prejean will clam up even more if

Agnes starts nagging. "Not another word," Agnes says. "At least today."

It's Wednesday and the art room is closed after school. Instead of sitting at a library table, Agnes decides to do her homework at the track so she can keep an eye on her friend.

Today in practice Prejean is running the 440. Agnes watches her crouch with her heel against the block. Mrs. Newton blows the whistle and off she goes, outdistancing three other girls for the first half, tying for first at the end. On her second round, she slows down to a hop-walk before the lap is through. Pinching her side, Prejean sits down on a bench and puts her head between her knees.

Agnes stands, ready to run over there herself, when Mrs. Newton beats her to it. Prejean, breathing heavily, points to her stomach. The coach hands her some bottled water and sits down beside her.

As Agnes watches them talk, she wonders if she should say something to Mrs. Newton in private. Would that be breaking a promise? After all, didn't Prejean promise to start eating? And if she broke a promise to Agnes, is Agnes still obligated to Prejean?

Agnes believes that if Prejean hadn't been in the bathroom stall today, she probably would have spilled all her worries to Natalie Kim. If only Agnes could lean on her mother. Mrs. Parker would know what to do.

Last year, Agnes prided herself on loyalty to her friend. It seems that in sixth grade, friends and promises were easier to keep.

CHAPTER SEVEN

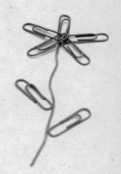

For the next few days, Prejean's mood changes. She doesn't pick fights. She doesn't even talk all that much.

"Have you written your speech yet?" Agnes asks on the drive to school.

"I've written five," says Prejean. "And I've erased five."

"Isn't tomorrow the election?" Mrs. Parker asks.

"Uh-huh." Prejean leans her head against the window.

"I can help you if you want," Agnes offers. "It'd be fun."

Prejean exhales and watches the passing traffic. "Fun," she says.

Agnes is reminded of the time she caught a frog in a creek and put it in a plastic carton. At first, it was a happy, hoppy, regular frog. The next day, though, when she took off the lid and peeked in, the frog looked a lot like Prejean does now. When Agnes put it back in the water, it was too late. All the hop had gone out of the frog forever.

In art class, Aram must sense that Agnes is preoccupied. He sits beside her and works quietly on the Cornell box that he has designed to look exactly like a Horace Mann school locker.

"Aren't you going to tell me any crazy stories today?" Agnes asks.

"Excuse me," says Aram, "but you hurt me. I've never told you anything that wasn't completely true."

"Well, I've got one for you," Agnes says. "I knew a girl once who had this ferocious appetite. Whenever she went to the drive-thru she always got the combo with two cheeseburgers."

"I'm hoping there's more to this," Aram says gravely. "Or you disappoint me."

"One day she stopped eating. And not only did her body get all skinny, but her personality got so shrunken, you could fit it in your Cornell locker box and still have room for that gigantic backpack of yours."

"You are the perfect weight for your height, I hope you know," says Aram. "Although your feet are a little big."

"Thanks," says Agnes, "but I'm not talking about me."

✱ ✱ ✱

After class, she tries to persuade Prejean to avoid taking the back stairs, where the eighth-grade boys are hanging out.

"This is the way I always go to World History," says Prejean, "and I'm not a wuss. If you don't want to be seen with me, it won't hurt my feelings."

"This has nothing to do with not wanting to be seen with you, Prejean," Agnes says. But Prejean pushes on.

Both girls crush themselves to the side of the crowded stairwell and climb. "Do you hear that?" Agnes asks. "It sounds like someone's mooing."

"It's Shane," says Prejean. "And he's booing."

Agnes can now glimpse Shane and Rex McNeeny standing with their hands cupped around their mouths. The "Booooooo!" is directed at Prejean, who stands very straight and pretends not to notice.

In contrast, Agnes can feel her shoulders tensing. She hugs her pile of books like a teddy bear. When a spit wad of wet paper hits Prejean's cheek and another sticks to Agnes's ear, however, she wells up with such sudden anger that she scares herself. She pictures herself whacking Shane with her biology textbook and pushing him down the stairs.

"You're disgusting!" she cries.

Laughter is all she hears in response.

When they arrive at Prejean's class, Agnes checks

77

her hair for more spit wads. "I don't care if I'm late for bio," Agnes says. "I need soap and I need it now."

"I'm sorry, Agnes," Prejean says.

"It's not your fault," Agnes assures her.

"What I mean is, I'm sorry . . . about everything." She shakes her head. "You worked so hard. And I know that tomorrow, I'm toast."

"That's not true," Agnes says. "You can do it. Write the speech today, and tomorrow it'll be over. No need to give up. Yet."

Prejean picks a wet piece of paper off the top of Agnes's head. "Missed one," she says.

At lunch, Agnes grabs an extra Jell-O and a roll and sits down by Prejean. She pulls out a sharpened pencil and a piece of lined paper and talks slowly.

"Here's the plan," she states. "The Jell-O is squishy and easy to eat. You are going to spoon it into your mouth while I, your secretary, will write down the words to your speech." She watches Prejean and the bowl of Jell-O. "You first," Agnes says.

Prejean, looking determined, picks up the quivering red stuff and closes her mouth around the spoon.

"Swallow," says Agnes. And Prejean does.

Agnes's pencil is poised to write. "Let's start with something simple," Agnes says. "How about, 'Good morning'?"

Prejean clears her throat. "Good morning . . ." she begins. Then Brian Olansky butts in.

"Natalie told me what happened today in the stairwell," he says. "It must be true too, because everyone's talking about it. How you doing, Prejean?"

"She's doing okay. In fact," Agnes says pointedly, "she's busy writing her speech for tomorrow."

"You got guts," Brian says. "I mean it. You've got all of the eighth-grade boys against you."

"This is a seventh-grade election. We're not worried about the eighth-grade boys because they don't vote," Agnes says.

"I know. But it can't be a *good* thing, can it?"

"You're giving them way too much credit. No one cares." Agnes tries to burn a hole in Brian's head with her forceful stare. "After all, I'm sure you're still voting for Prejean. Aren't you, Brian?"

"Me? Yeah." Brian looks both ways, then speaks out of the side of his mouth. "But I'm not letting any of the guys know it."

Agnes reaches under the table and sharply pokes Brian's leg.

"Ow," he says. "What did you do that for?"

Prejean pushes away her bowl. "Thanks for the report, Brian. Now if you guys don't mind, I'm going to sit in the library until I come up with some sort of speech."

Brian waves cheerfully as Prejean stands and leaves. "No problem!" he calls after her.

Agnes eyes the abandoned Jell-O. "Brian Olansky, I want to kill you," she says.

"Wha?"

"Never mind," Agnes says, shaking her head.

She is not surprised to find that Prejean still hasn't finished her speech when school ends.

"I'll come up with something," promises Prejean. "You worry too much."

"Yeah, about *you*," Agnes says. She finds some comfort in knowing that at least tomorrow the whole election thing will be over. Maybe with the pressure off, Prejean can try eating, do a little running on the side, and start being normal again.

But Friday morning is anything but normal. Agnes is dashing downstairs for breakfast when she hears the flutey beep of their rarely-used fax machine. She stands over it and watches as it spits out a paper lined with Prejean's straight-up-and-down printing.

Good morning, teachers and seventh graders, the first line says.

Then the phone rings. She picks it up. "Hello?"

"Agnes, this is Mrs. Duval."

"Oh no," says Agnes.

"Pardon?" says Mrs. Duval.

"Is Prejean all right?"

"No, dear," says Mrs. Duval. "Prejean is sick. That's why I'm calling . . ."

Agnes can hardly listen as Prejean's mother describes her daughter's stomach pain and last night's visit to the hospital. Agnes's mind is flooded with scenes of doctors in surgical masks sadly pointing to X-rays of Prejean's skeleton.

"If it's a disease, please tell me," Agnes pleads.

"It's an ulcer, Agnes," says Mrs. Duval. "It's an inflammation in the stomach."

Tears well up and spill down Agnes's cheeks. "Will she be okay?"

"Oh dear, please don't cry," Mrs. Duval says, her voice gentle. "I don't want to scare you, darling. It's what they call stress-related. They have medicine for it."

"Good." Agnes wipes her face on her sleeve and takes a deep breath. "So what about the election?"

Mrs. Duval pauses. "Obviously, I'm trying to spare Prejean all the stress I can. I tried to tell her that it's no disgrace to drop out. But you know my daughter."

"She's not coming to school today, is she?"

"Absolutely not," Mrs. Duval says. "But she asks that you please read her speech today if you can."

Agnes glances down at the fax machine and groans.

"I sent a copy to you," says Mrs. Duval.

"I got it," Agnes says, now feeling saturated with gloom.

"Now, now," says Mrs. Duval, "don't be upset, Agnes. You don't have to do it. Prejean already told me to tell you that she'll understand if you're too scared."

Agnes straightens. "Scared?" she repeats.

"Or maybe she said 'shy.' In any case, don't feel pressured, dear."

Agnes promises not to feel pressured. Then, as soon as she hangs up, she flies upstairs to her parents' bedroom. The shower is running. "Mom!" Agnes shouts through the door.

"It's just me!" answers Mr. Parker.

Agnes throws back her head and wails, then flops down on her parents' unmade bed.

Mrs. Parker, still in her bathrobe, rushes into the room.

"I heard shrieking all the way downstairs. Did you want me?"

"Mom, Prejean has an ulcer . . ."

"My goodness!"

"And I think it's partly my fault."

Mrs. Parker sits down. "Why don't we start from the beginning?" she says.

Agnes tells her everything—about the Duvals' separation, about Prejean's stomach. "I knew she was sick, but I didn't know with what. If I'd told Mrs. Duval earlier, maybe she'd be okay right now."

"You were in a tough situation," Mrs. Parker says. "You tried to do the right thing."

"I tried to make her eat Jell-O," Agnes says. "I spent hours pushing her campaign. And now I'm telling you things I shouldn't. It's hard to know when to get involved." Agnes sighs. "Especially today." She shows her mother Prejean's speech.

"Poor Prejean," says Mrs. Parker. "What a shame. She's going to miss out, I guess."

"Yes, but she asked me to be her stand-in. Ack! They're going to make me talk into a microphone! Why can't *I* have the ulcer?"

"Take that back," says Mrs. Parker.

"Strep throat? A case of the flu?"

"Agnes . . ."

"All right. I wish I was invisible." Agnes leans into her mother's shoulder.

Mrs. Parker speaks softly. "Agnes, sweetie, if it's too much, you don't have to do it."

Agnes stiffens. "That's what Prejean said."

"Well," continues Mrs. Parker, "she offered you an out. That was thoughtful, don't you think?"

Agnes pulls away and folds her arms around herself. She feels vaguely ashamed.

"I'm going to do it," she says.

"Really?"

Agnes notes that her mother looks truly surprised.

83

"Absolutely!" she declares, as if she were never in doubt.

There's a knock from inside the bathroom. "Can I come out now?" Mr. Parker asks politely. "I need pants."

Mrs. Parker looks at her watch. "Agnes! We better start hopping," she says. "Look, if you hustle downstairs and toast some bagels, I'll hurry and get dressed."

"Right away," she says, although she would like nothing better in the entire universe than to stay nestled on her warm, familiar sofa and watch television for the next eight hours.

"Onward, Agnes Parker!" says her mother.

Agnes knows that look. It's Mrs. Parker's time-honored method of giving her daughter a confidence transfusion.

"Right!" says Agnes, pretending that it still works. "Onward!"

CHAPTER EIGHT

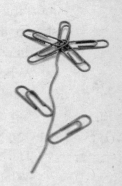

At first, Vice Principal Fairwether is baffled by Agnes's request to give Prejean's speech.

"I don't know that we've ever had this happen before. I'll have to consult Mr. Baines," she says. "Just to make sure there's no rule against it. He's our expert on student government."

While Mrs. Fairwether makes a call to the classroom, Agnes crosses her fingers behind her back.

She watches as a smile breaks out on the vice principal's face. "Uh-huh. That's great, Bob. I'll tell her . . ."

Agnes can feel herself deflate. "I'm going to have to give the speech, aren't I?"

Mrs. Fairwether's smile disappears. "Isn't that what you asked for?"

"Yes. Thank you," Agnes says, trying to sound sincere. "Prejean will be glad."

The election assembly is being held first thing this morning for Horace Mann seventh graders. Agnes is shown into the empty gym, where both Shane and Matthew wait on folding chairs.

"Who are you?" asks Matthew.

"I'm Prejean. Just for the assembly," says Agnes.

"What happened to her?" Shane asks with phony concern. "Did she decide to stay home?"

"Her doctor decided for her," Agnes says.

"What kind of doctor?" Shane circles his finger by his ear. "Her shrink?"

Agnes looks at Matthew to see if he's going to join in the Prejean bashing. But he's too busy studying his piece of paper and mumbling to himself.

"I didn't write anything down," Shane says, slouching in his chair.

"Why are you even running?" Agnes asks.

Matthew looks up from his speech. "Good question, Shane. I was wondering about that too."

"Because," Shane says, "it's a good way to get girls to know who you are. And also, I have fifty bucks riding on it. See, Cody and James both bet me twenty-five that I wouldn't stay in the race till the end. So, even if I lose, I win."

"Whatever," says Matthew. "Your loss is my gain."

"Or Prejean's gain," Agnes says.

Both boys look at her as if she's nuts.

"What?" Agnes says. "She's still in the race, you know."

Seventh graders begin to file in. With every row of bleachers that fills with kids, Agnes feels more nauseated.

"Matthew," Agnes whispers, "do you know how many seventh graders there are?"

"Four hundred sixty-seven," he says without looking up. "Ratio of boys to girls, 226 to 241."

"Wow," Agnes says.

"Breakdown from feeder schools: 112 from Woodlands, 110 from Oakview, 119 from Edison, and 126 from Inverness."

"Is this stuff we're supposed to know?" Agnes says. "Because I didn't study."

"These are the kind of facts I check into," Matthew says. "You might not be surprised to know I'm going to be in politics someday."

"I'm going to be an artist."

"Oh," Matthew says.

The way he looks at her, Agnes thinks she might as well have confessed that she has dandruff.

"As a matter of fact," she says, testing Matthew for a sense of humor, "I'm planning on being a starving artist. With paint stains on my tennis shoes. I'm going to live in an abandoned building without electricity. That's how Ms. Felson-Morales started out."

"Good luck with that," Matthew says sarcastically.

Agnes now can't decide which one she dislikes more, Shane or Matthew. Whoever comes in second place has to serve as vice president, and Agnes can't picture Prejean working with either one of these guys.

"Ready, folks?" Mr. Baines tests the dreaded microphone while the vice principal has the candidates draw straws to decide who speaks first.

"Me!" says Shane, holding up the short straw.

"Agnes will go next," says Mrs. Fairwether.

"Glad I'm not first," murmurs Agnes.

"Going last is actually the best," Matthew says, "in my opinion."

Mr. Baines taps the mike one last time. "Hello, seventh graders!" he says. "Please settle down. Our three fine candidates for class president have worked hard on their speeches and deserve your full attention."

Agnes notices Ashley holding up a Prejean sign. Natalie sits next to her, her mouth hanging open in surprise. Agnes gives a helpless shrug.

"First up, Shane McNeeny. Shane?" Mr. Baines lifts his hands high and leads the applause.

Shane strides forward, puts his lips on top of the microphone, and growls, "Hellll-o!"

This makes the crowd laugh. He then flings his arms in the air. "I WANT TO BE YOUR RULER!" he proclaims.

Some kids cheer while a large block of Blacker Backers hiss.

"YOUR HATE ONLY MAKES ME STRONGER!"

There's jostling in the bleachers as more kids stand up and roar. "McNeeeeneee!" booms a trio of his over-sized friends.

Agnes watches an unhappy Mr. Baines start from his chair. Shane sees him too.

"Good night, ladies and gentlemen!" Shane yelps. "Thank you very much!" He hastily seats himself, crosses his legs, and knots his hands in his lap.

Mr. Baines's head is lowered like a bull's. He looks up through his eyebrows. "Students," he says, "we demand your respectful attention. I expect complete silence until each candidate's speech is completed. Then and only then may you cheer and/or applaud. Do I make myself understood?"

He waits until Agnes can hear her own heartbeat in her ears.

"Better," he says. "Now, we have a slight change in program. Candidate Prejean Duval is ill today and her speech will be delivered by her campaign manager . . ." Mr. Baines covers the microphone and whispers, "What's your name again?"

Agnes's mouth is dry. "Agnes Parker," she rasps.

"Ann S. Harper," Mr. Baines announces, bowing. "Ann?"

Agnes has trouble picking up her feet as she walks. It's a long way to the microphone. When she arrives, she holds up Prejean's speech and steadies herself. It takes a while for her to notice that the deep, furnace-like roar echoing through the gym is the sound of her own nostrils breathing into the mike.

"Good morning, peachers. I mean teachers." The words on the page seem to be swimming. Agnes lifts the paper inches beneath her chin. "Good morning, *teachers* and *seventh* graders. I am Prejean Duval and I am running for change."

She clears her throat. "I decided to run for president when I noticed that many seventh graders are scared of their own school. In my case, I would like to be able to walk down the hall without a gang of boys shouting at me and grading my looks."

"Four!" someone yells from the bleachers.

Agnes flinches at the laughter. Mr. Baines pops out of his chair and shades his eyes, looking for the culprit.

"But that is not the only thing wrong with this school," Agnes resumes, concentrating on her paper. "Seventh-grade boys are scared of eighth-grade boys. Girls are scared of other girls making fun of them for all sorts of reasons. I don't know what I can do about it, except to talk about it out loud. Maybe then teachers will take it seriously too.

"My World History teacher is always slapping the

big map with a ruler and telling us that it doesn't matter what little things go on in our halls. All that really matters is what goes on in the big world. But I disagree. Our halls *are* our world. I think we should start here first. That's what I mean when I say I'm running . . ."

Agnes hears a clatter, a jingling, and dares to look up. From several directions, coins are rolling toward her on the wooden floor. Boys are hooting. A penny makes it all the way to the microphone, bumps against her shoe, and clonks on its side.

She finishes. ". . . That's what I mean when I say I'm running for change."

The audience doesn't seem to know whether to applaud, and Agnes stands frozen. Mr. Baines takes the microphone from Agnes. "What did I say, people? When I find the students responsible for this, I guarantee that you will be spending weeks after school in the opportunity room after a personal apology to Ann."

Shane gives Agnes a smile. "Get it?" he says. *"Change."*

Agnes studies her knuckles. For her, the election is over. The conversation is over. Her life as Ann S. Harper is over. Which is all fine with her.

Horace Mann Middle School, she thinks, *I gave you your chance . . .*

Matthew Blacker begins his speech by talking about fund-raising for new nets for the basketball hoops, then outlines his plan for monthly Hot Dog Day in the cafeteria. Agnes listens halfheartedly, knowing that this, after all, is the kind of thing class presidents always talk about. But does she care, really?

Sitting between Shane, the goof-off, and Matthew, the perfect presidential candidate, makes Agnes analyze how exactly she fits in with the seventh-grade scheme. She doesn't want to be bugged and singled out, but she doesn't want to go along, either. And joking aside, Agnes really does want to be someone brave enough to someday live in an abandoned building and paint through the night by a kerosene lantern—in theory. So what kind of girl should she be right now?

When the assembly is over, Natalie and Ashley run to Agnes.

"Agnes, that was awful." Ashley flings her hand over her heart. "I feel so sorry for you."

"Don't," says Agnes, walking quickly.

"What happened to Prejean?" asks Natalie.

"She's sick," says Agnes. "Her mother says she has an ulcer."

"I knew it!" Natalie says. "I knew something was wrong. Didn't I say that?"

Agnes wants to be instantly sitting in a corner chair in Ms. Felson-Morales's art room. "If you guys don't mind, I don't want to hang out and talk right now."

"I understand," says Ashley. "Soooo embarrassing."

Agnes spots Neidermeyer and Carmella making a beeline for her. "This is all I need," she says.

Neidermeyer, doing an Agnes imitation, goes knock-kneed and holds up a limp wrist: "G-g-good morning, *peachers*," she stutters. "Why did you say you were Prejean? Now everyone will think they're voting for *you*."

"Or not voting for her, more like," says Carmella.

"She was just reading the speech. People will know she's not Prejean," says Natalie.

"You *let* them throw *pennies* at you!" Neidermeyer says.

"Prejean would have at least said something," adds Carmella.

"Leave her alone!" says Natalie.

The girls are still arguing when Agnes ducks into Ms. Felson-Morales's room. She keeps a low profile and slips into her seat next to Aram.

"Miss A."

"Yes, Mr. A," Agnes says.

"Have I told you about my dog?"

"Nope."

"He is part wolf," Aram says. "With teeth like forks."

"Gee," Agnes says.

"I wished you had him up there with you today. I should have got permission to bring him. When he puts his lips back and shows the teeth, even criminals stop in their tracks."

"I wish I had him too," Agnes says. "I'd have made him give the speech. He probably would've done a better job."

Agnes feels someone's eyes on her. Ms. Felson-Morales is sitting at her desk with her chin in her hand, and she's smiling. She motions for Agnes to come over.

"Aren't you going to go?" Aram asks.

As nice as it is to have an invitation to talk, Agnes doesn't enjoy walking to the front of the class. She is sure everyone's eyes are glued to her. And when Ms. Felson-Morales has her take a seat at her desk, the silence in the classroom is especially notable. Plus, Brian Olansky is seated two feet away.

"Go ahead, you guys," says Ms. Felson-Morales to the class. "I'm sure you all have work to do." She pulls out two paper cups and pours some bottled water. "Join me?" she asks Agnes.

When Agnes takes the water, she sees that Ms. Felson-Morales is raising her cup in a toast.

"To Agnes Parker," she says. "Congratulations."

Agnes, reddening, takes a sip along with her teacher, then quickly sets the cup down.

"You know, Agnes," says Ms. Felson-Morales, "that was one of the best speeches I've heard here. And I've been at Horace Mann for nine years."

"It was Prejean's speech," Agnes says. "I just read a piece of paper." *Badly,* she thinks.

"But you delivered the message." Ms. Felson-Morales picks up her knapsack and takes out a little album. "I want to show you something," she says, opening the book. She points to two old school photographs. The bigger girl looks about sixteen, with shiny black curly hair, a direct gaze, and a bright smile. The little girl, on the other hand, has black hair that's been raked down clumsily over her forehead. Her chin recedes and her lips are clamped together. She stares off, not quite looking at the camera. "Guess which one I am."

The big girl has the strong jaw and curly hair of Ms. Felson-Morales. Agnes squints at the smaller girl until she realizes that this too is a picture of her teacher. "What happened to you?" Agnes asks.

"A lot of things have happened to me," she says. "But the first thing was, I was shy. I had this mad-scientist hair that I was always unsuccessfully gelling down. On top of that, I used to walk hunched over, looking at the ground. People used to call me Igor." Ms. Felson-Morales sips. "But actually some good things came out of that seventh-grade year . . ." She smiles.

"Like what?"

"That was the year I discovered watercolor. And I didn't do much during that year *but* watercolor. So you see, I got started on something very important to me."

"When's the other picture from?"

"I was seventeen and about to graduate high school," says Ms. Felson-Morales. "I had an art scholarship. I could see the light at the end of a very long tunnel."

Agnes feels a bit disappointed. "So what you're saying is, the tunnel lasts from seventh grade to senior year?"

"No!" says Ms. Felson-Morales. "Oh my goodness, no. You start seeing light before that."

"Then I don't get it," Agnes says.

"To me, the worst thing about being your age wasn't being rejected. It was, why don't the people I know ever talk about the things that matter? I knew everyone was worried about the same things, but they were always so guarded. It might not look like it to you, but at this age, every kid hides weakness very carefully. So here's the game everyone plays: The best diversion from *my* weakness is to point out *your* weakness."

Agnes can see some truth in this observation. "But not everybody does that," she says. "I don't and I never will."

"Well then, hold on to that, Agnes." Ms. Felson-Morales claps her on the shoulder and smiles. "When I decided to teach, I picked middle school just because this is when kids get so closed up. How crazy is that?"

"Actually," says Agnes, "if I were a teacher, I'd never come back. When I get out, I'm running."

"I know it feels as if that's the way to go," says Ms. Felson-Morales. "But can I let you in on something? For many people—and I say this from years of experience—it never gets any harder than it is right now in middle school."

Agnes believes this. But there are almost two years left at Horace Mann. And this is a monumentally horrible day. And it's only first period.

"Trust me," says Ms. Felson-Morales. "No matter how tough the going gets, the challenge is to go forward with an open heart."

"I will," Agnes says. When she stands, she notices that Brian Olansky has been eavesdropping.

"Good job, Agnes!" he says earnestly. "I mean it."

"You do?" Agnes asks.

"I'm sticking up for you," he says. "No matter what anyone says, you're not a loser."

Then and there, Agnes quietly decides to keep her heart closed for the foreseeable future.

CHAPTER NINE

These are the items that Agnes has pulled from her closet:

Everything with a heart or flower on it.

Everything that has color.

Everything that suggests her shape.

Everything that looks like a girl would wear it.

The only clothes left hanging are murky, baggy, hooded or black.

Then she throws herself across her bed and opens the first page of her first-ever journal.

Hello. I am Agnes Parker. I live at 333 Schuyler St. I hate Horace Mann Middle School. It is full of spiteful kids. I refuse to be friendly to any of them. Okay, maybe I plan to be nice to the following people:

My mom
My dad
Natalie and Ashley
Of course Prejean
Aram Keshishian
Ms. Felson-Morales

Anyone else must work very very very hard
to earn my respect. And if they don't,

(here Agnes raises her pen to her lips and considers)

they can spend the afterlife burning
wretchedly in eternal fire.

Those last words, borrowed from a TV preacher, feel like the right touch. Prejean would appreciate them.

Agnes doesn't bother to pick up her room before biking off to Prejean's. She's too anxious to have her best friend's company. Last night, she spent over an hour on the phone apologizing for screwing up the speech. Prejean claimed not to care anymore about the election—even if it meant coming in third behind Shane McNeeny. All she wants is to be able to eat again like a normal person.

As Agnes peddles up, she sees Prejean sitting on her front porch munching on a banana.

"You're eating!" Agnes says. "I wish I'd known. I would've brought barbecue potato chips."

"They aren't on my diet," says Prejean. "For now it's bananas, applesauce, and toast."

Agnes sits on the cold concrete. "Brrrr. It's really starting to feel like fall, isn't it?"

"And you're bundled up," Prejean says. "Actually, you look like you're dressed for a carjacking."

Agnes pulls up the hood on her baggy black sweatshirt. "I like it in here," she says.

"It's even warmer in the house," Prejean says. "You will not believe what happened today."

As the girls walk inside, Agnes sees Prejean's dad's golf clubs standing in the entryway along with a big nylon bag.

"Is somebody going someplace?" asks Agnes carefully. "Or coming back?"

"That's my dad's stuff. He brought everything home from the cabin." Prejean lowers her voice. "It's been sitting out here since early this morning and my mother hasn't said a thing."

"Is your dad back, then? For real?"

Prejean crooks a finger. "Let's go to my room," she whispers.

Agnes learns that Prejean's parents have finally talked to her about the separation. Her father said he should never have left without sitting down and talking to Prejean about it.

"I don't know if my stomach problems sped things up or what," Prejean says. "They say they're working things out."

"I'm so glad for you," Agnes says.

"Thanks," Prejean says. "But I don't trust it yet. I still think he might leave again."

"Why?"

"Because they're still not happy. I can feel it."

Agnes wishes the news were better. "Anything I can do for you, you know," she says.

"You already gave the speech." Prejean ducks her head. "That was awful of me to ask you. I've been feeling guilty about it."

"Don't," Agnes says.

"No, I shouldn't have put you through it. Even Natalie thinks so."

The thought of people discussing her humiliating performance behind her back makes Agnes bury her head in a pillow.

"Did I say something?" Prejean asks.

Agnes lifts her head and rests on her elbows. "I'd like to put this whole stupid election way behind us. I've been thinking about this a lot, and I've decided we should both drop out of society. Or school. Whatever you call it."

"Sure. We'll drop out of school," Prejean says, pretending to be serious. "Good plan."

"I don't mean drop out. I mean, let's just have our own group. We can ignore everyone else and be, like, the Untouchables."

"Who would we be allowed to touch, then?" Prejean asks.

"Natalie and Ashley. And for me, maybe Mr. A," Agnes says. "You can pick your own people too."

"Can I pick Derry and Valerie?"

"No," Agnes says firmly.

"Just kidding." Prejean wraps her arms around her knees and thinks. "I don't know who I'd pick. But I might as well join you. It's not like I have scads of people to choose from."

Agnes brightens. "We'll make dorkdom interesting."

"Precisely," says Prejean. "*Choose Dorkdom!* That can be our next campaign."

Then Mrs. Duval calls from down the hall. "Prejean!"

"Yes?" yells Prejean from the bed.

The door flings open. "For heaven's sake," she says, "don't yell through the door."

"You yelled through the door first," says Prejean.

Mrs. Duval wags a finger. "Do not be sassy, Prejean. I was busy and the least you can do is . . ."

At least Prejean and her mother are back to normal, Agnes thinks.

Mrs. Duval looks down as if she's forgotten she's carrying a phone in her hand. Quickly she covers the receiver. "It's for you!" she says. "It's a *boy*."

102

Prejean takes the phone and Mrs. Duval stands with her hands on her hips, watching.

"Hello? . . . Yep, it's me. . . : Uh-huh." Prejean sticks out her tongue. "It's Matthew Blacker," she tells Agnes.

"Matthew who?" asks Mrs. Duval, seemingly alarmed.

"It's okay, Mother. It's the guy who beat me for class president."

Mrs. Duval backs out. The way she says "Keep the door open" makes Agnes giggle.

Prejean listens intently. "Are you kidding?" she asks. "Whoopee," she says unenthusiastically. "Well, it isn't exactly an honor, ya know. But thanks for calling."

"What, what?" asks Agnes as Prejean hangs up.

"Shane McNeeny forfeited vice president. He said if he couldn't be president, he didn't want to do anything at all."

"He's lazy," Agnes says. "And he's a snot. And still I lost to him."

"No, *I* lost," says Prejean. "Fair and square."

"So wait," Agnes says. "Does that mean you're vice president now?"

Prejean nods. "I have to work with Matthew. There's a student council meeting on Monday." She pauses, then starts to laugh. "You know what's funny? *I* don't want to be vice president either."

"You should forfeit and give the job back to Shane,"

Agnes says. "You're supposed to be an outcast with me, remember?"

"What have I gotten myself into?" Prejean says.

"Don't blame me. I'm the crummy public speaker. I did my part."

"I bet he'll try to boss me around. Either that or he'll totally ignore me," Prejean says. "Which would be fine."

Agnes puts her fingers to her temples, psychic style. "I see you in matching aprons. I predict many happy Hot Dog Days ahead for both of you," Agnes says.

Prejean grabs a second pillow and whomps it down firmly on Agnes's head. "I'd *much* rather be an Untouchable," she says.

On the way to the car Monday morning, Mrs. Parker stops. "Sweetie," she says, "is this really what you're wearing to school today?"

"What's wrong with it?'" Agnes asks.

"The sweatshirt is a little big, don't you think? It looks like you're wrapped in a black cocoon."

"I *am* in a black cocoon," Agnes tells her. "That's the point."

When they pick up Prejean, however, Agnes is surprised to see her run out the door in a pink T-shirt.

"Pink?" says Agnes. "That's not what we said we'd wear."

"I thought it looked good with the black pants," Prejean says.

Yes, it does look good, Agnes thinks. Too good. There is nothing Untouchable about Prejean in this outfit.

"I think you're wearing this because you have student council today," Agnes says. "You want to look *good*."

Prejean looks down at her shirt. "You're acting like this is a glitter tank top or something. It's just a stupid T-shirt."

"According to Agnes, the point is to appear as if you are dressed in a black cocoon," Mrs. Parker says.

Her mother's teasing stings Agnes. "I'm glad you think I'm such a joke."

"Well," says Mrs. Parker, "pardon me. I didn't mean to . . ."

"Geez, Agnes," Prejean says. "Be nice."

"Easy for you. You're going back to school as vice president. I'm just the idiot people threw pennies at."

Stop, stop, Agnes tells herself. **Why am I being such a jerk?**

Neither Prejean nor Mrs. Parker speaks to Agnes for the rest of the ride.

"See you at lunch?" Agnes finally says as she and Prejean part in the hall.

"I have student council," Prejean says. "Remember?"

"How could I forget?" Agnes says, snarky again.

"Whatever!" says Prejean. "You are in a mood today, aren't you?"

Agnes continues the morning with a black cloud in her head. In art class, she looks over her almost-completed Cornell box with its flower garden theme and can't believe how dumb and clunky it looks. Daisies are planted like lollipops. It looks like a Barbie toy.

One by one, Agnes plucks out the little flowers she's spent a week painstakingly gluing.

"Why are you picking the flowers?" Aram asks.

"Because they're so goofy-looking," she says.

"I thought you said you wanted to put a garden in a box."

"I did."

"I thought you said you wanted to make it look like a dollhouse."

"Don't remind me."

Aram opens his Horace Mann locker replica. "Did you see what I added to mine? That's a birthday cake on the top shelf. It's made out of toothpaste."

"It's so realistic, Aram," Agnes says. "How many candles?"

"All fourteen," Aram says. "You can count them. And over here? This is a picture of my dog."

"This little thing? With the poofy tail? I thought you said it was part wolf."

"Yes. Part wolf, part Chihuahua-Pomeranian mix."

"Of course," Agnes says. "It's exactly the kind of dog you'd have."

"You mean because it's little?" Aram asks, sounding defensive.

"Yes, but with a wolf inside. You know what I mean. It's your symbol."

Surveying her own semi-destroyed box, Agnes wonders what's symbolic of herself. It's easy to tear apart what's been built, but how do you decide what to put in its place?

While Prejean is at student council, Agnes tries to sell the idea of the Untouchables to Ashley and Natalie.

"The idea is," explains Agnes, "we don't care what everyone thinks. We have our own group, and we hang together sort of in the shadows."

"And we're supposed to dress for the shadows too, I'm guessing," Natalie says, giving Agnes's baggy sleeve a tug.

"Yeah. This message is, we know we're dorks, and we like it that way."

"I'm a dork?" Ashley says. "Why do I want to be a dork?"

"What she's saying, I think," says Natalie, "is that if we don't try to be cool, and accept being *not* cool—that would be cool in itself." She scratches her head. "Do I even have that right?"

"Close," Agnes says. "Maybe I should re-explain what I mean by dork . . ."

"Maybe you should," says Ashley, doubtful.

"Hey Ashley," call Valerie and Derry in a unison singsong. "Whatcha doing?"

"Hey yourself," Ashley says, turning twinkly. "C'mon and sit down."

Agnes draws her baggy sweatshirt around herself. She had heard from Natalie that Ashley was spending almost half her time with these two. Now it was definitely beginning to show.

"Me and Derry and Valerie went shopping at Urban Girl yesterday," Ashley says.

"And we could not be-*lieve* how *ug*-ly the clothes are there!" declares Derry.

Valerie looks at Agnes and does a double take. "Ohmigosh," she says. "Is that you? I totally did not know who you were!"

"Yes. It's me," says Agnes.

"Agnes was just telling us about a new group she's starting," Ashley explains. "She wants us to be dorks with her."

"Say again?" says Derry, cupping her ear.

"Oh gawd," says Valerie. "Did you sign up?"

Agnes watches as Ashley swivels uncertainly between Agnes and the Derry/Valerie group. "Not yet," she says.

"Now, that's not exactly right," Natalie says. "Agnes isn't asking us to sign up."

"Good!" says Derry. "Because I'm pretty for sure certain that would qualify as . . . "

"...PSYCHO!" finishes Valerie.

"Anyway! I was joking," says Agnes. "It was a *joke*, Ashley."

"Oh," Ashley says, looking relieved. "Right! Ha!"

"Ha. Dork club. Like I was serious . . ." Agnes stands. "Must go now," she says, picking up her tray.

"Bye, Agnes," Natalie says.

There's something sorrowful in the way she says it, Agnes thinks. Their little group from Woodlands Elementary feels a lot less solid all of a sudden.

What could Ashley see in Derry and Valerie? The idea of sharing Agnes's plan with them seems disloyal. The whole idea of the Untouchables was to retreat and observe—to be outcasts *together*.

She can think of nowhere to go now except the restroom. In her hurry, she forgets to check the halls first for safety. Rounding a corner, Agnes finds herself smacking into Shane McNeeny—who in turn is attached to the entire eighth-grade boy gang.

"Aaaaaah!" Shane screams and recoils like a kid in a horror movie.

Agnes freezes. The boys seem to move in slow motion as they shove their hands into their pockets.

She knows what's coming. She runs, hearing the rolling clatter of pennies behind her.

When Agnes reaches the bathroom, she pushes open the door and flees to a stall. There's a big question she hasn't considered, and now she feels sickened by doubt.

Does she have what it takes to be an outcast all by herself?

CHAPTER TEN

Is there a song about the way I feel? If I could find one I'd play it all the time . . .

Agnes, waiting for her ride home after art room duty, sits on the bleachers and shivers as she writes in her journal. Sometimes she pauses to blow on her hands. Prejean, meanwhile, has worked up a sweat with her repeated trips around the track. Every day she ends up finishing a little bit later.

And this routine has gone on for weeks. At first, Prejean would wave at Agnes when she did an exceptionally fast sprint. But now she turns to the other runners and talks. Right now, three other girls are standing bent with their hands on their knees, laughing with Prejean about something Agnes can't make out.

Prejean, with her stomach on the mend and her parents on good behavior, is warming up to all the seventh-grade stuff. She didn't even seem to mind skipping trick-or-treating this year. For one thing, Prejean wasn't well enough to stuff herself with candy, and both girls agreed that they were probably too old to go around in costume. But every time the doorbell rang that night, Agnes felt as she had when she lost her stuffed rabbit on vacation. Something precious, irreplaceable, was missing.

People seem so far away sometimes, like I'm looking in the wrong end of the binoculars . . .

There's a funny sensation she has right now. Something like the gnawing of an empty stomach, only lower. And everything about the athletic field—the line of bunged-up chain-link fence, the puddles left over from yesterday's rain—makes her feel like the focus of the entire world's loneliness.

She rifles through her backpack looking for something to stuff in her mouth and distract her from this slog. There's one grape Life Saver left in a bit of crumpled foil.

"Blech," she says. "My absolute unfavorite flavor."

Agnes slowly makes her way to the field's unheated restroom with its unfriendly smell of concrete, sweat, and toilet water. She hangs her backpack on the hook inside of the bathroom stall and undoes the button on her oversized army pants.

"Oh my gawd."

Agnes has gotten her period. Her first.

What to do? She checks her watch. Fifteen minutes until Mrs. Duval picks them up. She jingles her pockets and finds only two nickels and a penny. Not the right change for the pad machine.

Methodically, she winds toilet paper around her hand, then sticks the wad down her pants. Trying not to waddle, she makes her way to the bench, and feels as if she's sitting on a nest.

She watches the lanky Prejean, running around free. Normally, this is the type of thing Agnes would confide right away. But she doesn't feel like talking just now. And besides, Prejean hasn't started hers. It's not like she has any information.

This is the first day of something, Agnes writes in her journal (cryptically, in case someone ever finds it). Another kind of life? Remember this the way it was: cloudy, cold, and sitting on a metal bench. I can only hope it gets better from here . . .

Prejean has finally thrown a towel over her shoulder

"Thank goodness," says Agnes. "Home . . ."

Not yet. Prejean must wave good-bye to her track mates. Then Matthew Blacker jogs across the field from intramural football and stops Prejean again.

When Prejean does make it over to her shivering friend, she's flushed and twittery.

"That's the third day in a row he's come over to bug me," Prejean says.

113

"He's a ginormous pest, isn't he?" Agnes says.

"I guess," Prejean says. "Anyway, I told him on the first day of student council that he might have beaten me for president, but he'll never beat me on the track."

"And I suppose he had a fit," Agnes says. "Mr. I-Am-the-Winner."

"He actually wants to race!" Prejean says. "I told him, 'You're on.'"

"You sound so perky. Don't he and his people hate your guts?"

"It's the Shane people who hate me. The Matthew people won, so what do they care?" Prejean looks out at the football field. "This time, I'm going to smoke him. You'll see."

If Agnes were to be honest, she'd say she sort of misses the troubled, cranky Prejean. She pictures herself sitting on the bench, watching Prejean and Matthew tease and sweat and sprint while Agnes sits, forlorn, on her ungainly maxi pad.

"I just started my period," Agnes states.

"Huh?" says Prejean. "When?"

"Just now. It struck. Like lightning."

"How do you feel?"

"Grumpy," says Agnes.

"So nothing's changed," Prejean says, giving Agnes a gentle slug on the arm.

"No," says Agnes pointedly. "*Everything's* changed."

Prejean drops her smile and sits on the bleacher at Agnes's feet. "You're mad at me," she says.

"Not mad."

"Yes you are. I can feel it."

Agnes could lie and say no, but she decides to let that remark hang.

Prejean nods. "I knew it. Because I'm not acting like an *Untouchable,* right? Well, sorry. Sometimes I feel like you think I'm not supposed to be happy."

The way Prejean sinks her shoulders makes Agnes feel bad. It's as if Prejean's happiness really has just leaked out of her. "Don't say that," Agnes tells her.

"Would it make you feel better if I told you that I'm *not* happy? Because I'm still feeling awful when I'm alone. It's still not easy for me, Agnes."

"Things bad at home still?"

"Just icky." Prejean gestures to the field. "I like it better out here."

"Sorry," Agnes says. "I thought everything must be healing. I mean, you seem to run around and smile a lot."

"Well, you know me. I can't sit still and think about things. It makes everything worse."

"And you know me," Agnes says. "I'd rather be alone in a room with the door shut."

"Hey, maybe that's PMS," says Prejean.

"No, I think it's just plain old APS—Agnes Parker Syndrome."

"I wish I had Agnes Parker Syndrome sometimes," Prejean says. "I do run around to make myself feel better, but honestly? I just need to exhaust myself."

Agnes puts her hand on the top of Prejean's head. "One thing in my favor," says Agnes. "At least I'm not sweaty all the time."

"See? Even more extra points for you," says Prejean. "You definitely smell better than I do."

Agnes plugs her nose. "And here you said you're not an Untouchable."

Mrs. Parker is businesslike about Agnes's period news, which makes her daughter grateful. Agnes wonders if maybe the period is responsible for the creative black hole she's been in. Algebra is quickly becoming her subject of choice, with its puzzles and perfect balance of numbers on each side of the equation.

In art class the next day, Brian Olansky walks by and knocks on Agnes's still-empty Cornell box.

"Hello?" he says. "Any art in there?"

"No," says Agnes.

"Mine's done," he says. "I'm bored."

"Could you be bored back over in your own seat?" Agnes says.

"Touchy," says Brian.

Agnes turns the box over so she won't have to gaze into its emptiness.

"Are you wishing you didn't tear out the flowers?" asks Aram.

"As a matter of fact, yes," she says.

"Would you like me to help you put them back in?" he asks simply.

Agnes blinks. Then blinks again. Her eyes are filling with tears. She presses the cuff of her sweatshirt to her face. "Oh, this is so embarrassing," she says.

"It's no big deal," Aram says. "For me to cry, that would be a big deal. You girls have it easy."

"I threw all the flowers away and now I have no ideas. I'm stupid."

"We can make new ones," Aram says. "We'll draw them as fast as we can. They will all look sloppy and we don't care."

"Aram, no matter what I come up with now, it's going to be sloppy. I've only got two days to finish." Agnes vows to come back after school and fill up the box. "Gum wrappers, anything," she says. "I'll think of something by three thirty."

But after putting in a day at school, Agnes is still at a loss. She pulls out some colored papers from her backpack, places them on the table, and sits in the empty art room, hypnotized by the hum of the fluorescent lights.

"Yoo-hoo." Aram is peeking around the door.

Agnes is so happy to see him, she could hug him, almost. "Yoo-hoo to you too."

"I am here to help." He sits beside her and surveys the table. "What are you waiting for? The paper won't make itself into things on its own."

"This has never happened to me before," Agnes confesses. "I have never, ever been stuck for ideas when it comes to art. It's like my brain is drying up and I'm not even thirteen." She drops her head in her hands.

"Pick up scissors," Aram says. "Watch me."

Agnes watches and picks up scissors too.

"Now start cutting out a flower. One, two, three, go!"

Aram tears into a piece of paper and Agnes does too. When they're done, they compare their work.

"We have created two mutant daisies," Agnes says. "Now what?"

Aram thinks. His eyes spring wide open. "We will put faces on them!" he barks. "Go!"

Agnes grabs a colored pencil and starts scribbling.

"Done!" says Aram. His daisy has spirals for eyes and a tongue hanging out. "My flower is recovering from a bad car accident. SUV roll-over. You?"

Agnes looks at her flower, which appears open-mouthed and frightened. "My flower is facing down the front tire of a mountain bike driven by Peggy Neidermeyer."

"Okay. Go!" Aram says again, cutting crazily. "You should see the flower I'm making, Agnes. It has a flat head and a tremendously big butt."

"That's nothing," says Agnes, slamming down her flower and grabbing a pencil. "Mine's getting an eye patch and skin allergies."

The flowers pile up. As soon as they've drawn and described one flower's tale of woe, Aram yells "Go!" and the process starts over. By the end of the hour they have flowers on fire, flowers in handcuffs, flowers recovering from heart transplants and head colds. None are what you'd call pretty.

"We have enough here for an entire flower hospital," Agnes says, laughing.

"I'd rather call it THE FLOWER HOUSE OF MISERY," Aram says.

"Whatever you call it," says Agnes, "I say it's an artistic masterpiece."

"Me too," says Aram.

All Agnes has left is the gluing. "I thought I'd never finish. How can I thank you, Mr. A?"

"There is one way," he declares. "Come over for soup."

Agnes sees that Aram is serious. "Uh, I don't know."

"You can come tomorrow when the art room is closed," Aram says. "Then you won't sit out on the bench."

"It's so cold out there," Agnes says. "I thought my fingers would freeze yesterday."

"I know," Aram says. "That's why I feed you soup."

"I'll see," Agnes says. "I totally owe you. I should be the one feeding *you*."

Agnes gathers up her flowers and meets Prejean by the curb.

"Guess what?" says Prejean. "I ran the four forty today with Matthew. And I did beat him by a hair."

"Wow," Agnes says with mock admiration.

"No, really, Agnes, this is a big deal. He's very athletic. I pushed myself and got my best time ever." Prejean beams. "I'm really good at this running thing," she says.

"You say that like you're surprised," Agnes says.

"I am. You've always been the one with the talent."

Agnes sees that Prejean states this as a fact, not a compliment, and it makes her feel both flattered and embarrassed at the same time.

"Well, you're talented too. I'm not surprised you beat him," Agnes says. "I hope you shrunk his big, oversized head."

"If he won, I was supposed to go to that winter dance thing with him." Prejean searches Agnes's face. "Can you believe that?"

"No," Agnes says calmly. "I hope you got something for winning?"

"I got him to call a meeting with the teachers about the eighth-grade boys." Prejean grins. "Isn't that great?

It's what I wanted out of being president in the first place."

"And you don't have to dance with him," Agnes says.

"That too," Prejean says.

But not very enthusiastically, thinks Agnes.

At night upstairs in her room, Agnes spreads out her new collection of paper flowers on the bed and can't keep a smile off her face.

"Aram is so much fun," she says out loud. He's as easy to be with as Prejean. She can picture having him overnight and watching *Vandela's Horror Theater,* just like he was a girl or something. *I wonder what kind of pajamas he wears?*

In a way, it's dumb how the world divides people into boys and girls. Some people are meant to be friends, that's all. He's an art guy. He lurks around in dark corners, like Agnes. Come to think of it, Aram is a perfect co-Untouchable. They could have their own private club!

She catches a glimpse of herself in the mirror. Is that happy face really hers? For the first time she can remember, Agnes believes that going to school tomorrow might not be so bad.

CHAPTER ELEVEN

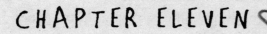

Agnes doesn't tell Prejean she's going to Aram's after school. She lets her think she's finishing her art project, instead. This new sense of secrecy makes her feel adventurous.

"Have fun running your little heart out," says Agnes. "I'll meet you at the curb in front of the school."

"For once, I wish I was going to the art room with you," Prejean says. "It feels like winter out here."

Aram spends the walk to his house preparing Agnes for what to expect at the Keshishians.

"My mother is, how to say it? . . . She is very *excited* about meeting you."

"That's nice," Agnes says. "I'm excited to meet her too."

"Not as excited as she is," Aram says. "She has made you dolma *and* blor kufta abour."

"Made me what?"

"Soup and—vine leaves. You know," he says. "Leaves from the grape?"

"I'm sure I'll love it," Agnes assures him.

"I hope," Aram says. "When I began school at Oakview Elementary, I brought lavash and basterma for lunch. Everybody but Edwin kept asking, 'What is it? What's that smell?' It embarrassed me."

"How rude," Agnes says.

"We stopped bringing lunch. Edwin and I eat the cafeteria things, even though my mother cooks beautiful food. Just so everyone will be quiet."

Aram's house is very modern on the outside—all stained wood and big glass windows. But inside, there are many old-fashioned touches. The dining table is covered in crocheted lace, a collection of little china cups lines one wall, and the furniture is overstuffed and cozy.

The tiny dog Agnes saw in Aram's photograph is now running in circles, yipping sharply. "Hush, Razmig!" Aram says. But the dog is too overjoyed to stop.

At the sound of barking, a petite woman in an apron hurries out from the kitchen. Her gaze is serious, like Aram's, even when she smiles. "Hello," she says.

"Agnes, my mother," says Aram.

"Glad to meet you," says Agnes.

Aram's mother nods, then turns to her son and speaks to him in Armenian.

"She says to take off your coat, come to the kitchen, and sit down. Do you like coffee?"

Before Agnes can answer, Aram adds, "I told her you don't drink it. But she has to ask."

Aram and Agnes sit in the little kitchen as Mrs. Keshishian ladles out what looks to be a meatball soup. She folds her arms and watches as Agnes takes her first sip.

"It's good," Agnes says. "What's the flavor in the meatball?"

Aram asks his mother, then translates.

"It's mint," he says.

Agnes gives Mrs. Keshishian a thumbs-up. "Good!" she says loudly.

Aram chuckles. "You think she'll understand English when you speak LIKE THIS!"

"That was dumb, huh?" says Agnes.

"It always happens," says Aram. "Let me tell you what drives me crazy. Every time something comes in the mail, I don't care if it is an ad for cleaning the carpet, if it comes in an envelope, I have to read the whole thing out loud to my parents in Armenian."

"That doesn't sound so bad," Agnes says.

"No, it is bad. I will say to them, you don't have to read this. It's not important. I beg them. But they don't want to miss anything. So ask me about the going-out-of-business sale at Mattress Heaven." Aram slaps

124

his forehead and sighs. "I read *everything*."

Agnes finishes the soup in no time, and Mrs. Keshishian is there at her elbow refilling the bowl. The dolmas Aram talked of earlier—grape leaves rolled around a tangy rice filling—are heavenly.

"When you can't eat anymore," Aram says, "tell me. Otherwise she will keep feeding you. She does not know how to stop."

Agnes keeps eating and sipping until she's sure she'll burst.

"Do you give up?" Aram asks. "Because I do."

"Yes," Agnes says, blotting her lips with a napkin. "But make sure you tell her thank you and that I think her cooking is fabulously delicious."

Aram tells his mother and a look of quiet pride suffuses her face.

"You're welcome," she says in English.

"Now, I'm going to show you something," Aram says. "Tell me what you think."

Agnes follows Aram to his room, where one wall is tacked all over with pencil sketches.

Some are landscapes with castles built into the side of rocks. Others show fantastically tall skyscrapers that narrow to tiny needles at the top. The style is part cartoon, part realistic.

"These are great," Agnes says. "How long have you been drawing them?"

"I've wanted to be an architect for a long time," Aram says. "These are my latest."

Agnes stops in front of one picture that shows not a building, but a starkly beautiful mountain.

"That is Mount Ararat. In Armenia. Noah's Ark is there, you know."

"Cool," she says. "So why did you guys move?"

"To save our lives," Aram says.

"You're kidding. What happened?"

"War happened," Aram says. "Not to me, but to my great-great-grandparents. They were thrown from their country and many of their friends and other family were killed. That's why so many Armenians aren't from Armenia anymore."

"I thought that was where you're from."

"No. My parents are Persian Armenian. Their families moved to Iran a long time ago. Some went to Lebanon. The ones who stayed in their home had a giant earthquake. This is when my parents were teenagers. A lot of them moved here to the U.S."

"So, have you ever been to Armenia?"

"Not yet," Aram says. "Only to Tehran to visit my grandparents. They stayed when the Ayatollah took over Iran, but my parents got out when I was two. Another bad thing. So we are even more scattered."

"Do you think that's what makes you want to build things?" Agnes asks.

126

"Part of it, maybe. I never thought of it."

Agnes turns to the other side of the room. Above a neatly made bed, there is a single poster for the Detroit Pistons.

"This must be your brother's side," Agnes says.

"Vrej," Aram says. "He is not into history. He's into basketball."

There's a picture on his dresser of a boys' basketball team. "Which one is Vrej?"

"Center," Aram says. "With the ball under his arm."

Agnes picks up the photo. "This one?" She can make out traces of Aram in Vrej's eyes and mouth, but Vrej looks twice as tall. He's staring directly into the camera, and soft black bangs fall over one brow. No doubt about it: He is what Agnes's mother would call "dreamy."

When Agnes looks up from the picture, she starts. There, standing in the doorway, is Vrej. He's posed exactly as he is in the team picture, complete with basketball under arm and soulful stare.

She wants to drop the picture—now—but all her body parts are glued in place.

"Hey," Aram says. "You're back early."

"Yeah," Vrej says. "We got bumped for a JV game."

Agnes is surprised, disappointed actually, that he doesn't sound like Aram at all. He sounds like a jock.

"Mom told me you had a friend over," Vrej says, pointing to Agnes. "But this definitely isn't Edwin."

127

"Say hi to Agnes," Aram says.

"Hi, Agnes." He sits on the bed and flips the basketball over his shoulder. It lands squarely in the laundry basket.

"Here's your picture," she says dumbly.

"Thanks," he says. "Aram, this is the first time a girl has ever been in this room. I tell you, you're Mom's favorite." Vrej leans back, his hands behind his head.

"He always says I'm the favorite," Aram confirms.

"Ohmigosh," Agnes says suddenly. "I have to meet Prejean at the curb."

"I will walk with you," Aram says.

"Bye," Vrej says.

"Bye," says Agnes. Vrej is like Aram plus twelve inches, but minus the funny personality. Is it possible that Aram will be that good-looking in two years? Imagine Aram's fabulous weirdness combined with the looks of Vrej. Agnes feels suddenly hopeful before she pushes the thought to the back of her mind.

"You should come back again," Aram says. "Tomorrow, after we clean the art room."

"I know," says Agnes. "I should."

"It's the first time I have been serious with you. It wasn't that bad," he says.

"It was fun, really."

"Something you should know. Now that we're serious."

Aram clears his throat. "Every day I walk Razmig, I see you over there on the bench. The one time I saw you blowing on your hands to keep warm, I decided to make sure that didn't happen again."

"But it was nothing. I wasn't freezing or anything," Agnes says.

"Someone like you shouldn't be alone so much. You are too nice and good."

"I think the same about you."

"Even though I'm not a basketball player?"

"I don't care about basketball," she says.

"Even though I am shorter than you?"

"I don't care about short!" Agnes declares.

"Good." He lowers his head and looks up through his lashes. "I will see you tomorrow."

Slowly, a smile spreads across his face.

Agnes has never seen that smile. It makes her want to hurry up. "Okay," she says. "Tomorrow."

When she reaches the curb, Mrs. Duval's car is there with the engine idling.

"Where have you been?" Prejean asks. "I just checked the art room."

"Sorry, I got involved in a conversation."

"It's all right. I've been making you wait for me for weeks."

"We'll be back to our regular schedule soon," says Mrs. Duval.

Prejean seems gloomy. "There's hardly any more track left. We break up after Thanksgiving."

The way Prejean says "break up" makes Agnes think her friend is talking about more than just running.

"You still have student council," Agnes says.

"Uh-huh," Prejean says. "I like to keep busy, that's all."

You are so obvious, Agnes thinks.

Agnes spends dinnertime comparing the meal at Aram's to her own at home. Nothing on the table is at all related to where Agnes's family comes from. They're eating pesto and pasta. Are they Italian? No. Last night her mom stir-fried chicken and vegetables in a wok.

"Mom, you're part Czech, right?"

"She's part Moravian," says Mr. Parker. "Her great-grandmother used to insist on that."

"Czechoslovakia is what Moravia turned into," explains Mrs. Parker. "And now Czechoslovakia is divided into two different countries."

"What do Moravians eat?" Agnes asks.

"I don't know," says Mrs. Parker.

"My family is Anglo Irish and we ate a lot of canned soup with crackers," Mr. Parker says. "I grew up on chicken noodle and saltines and tuna sandwiches." He takes a bite of pasta. "But then again, so did the German kids on the next farm over."

130

"That's so boring. When we come to America, why do we turn into mush?"

"It's possible to keep your identity even here," says Mrs. Parker. "Look at the Amish or the Orthodox Jewish people."

"The rest of us just bump around and fall in love and mix it up," says Mr. Parker. "More or less."

"And turn into mush people, like the Parkers," Agnes's mom says.

"Mush people," Agnes repeats. "That is so perfect."

That night, in the dark, Agnes thinks about Horace Mann Middle School as the gigantic Mush Factory. It's taking everyone and teaching them the do's and don'ts of mush people. Derry and Valerie are mush police. The eighth-grade boys are trying to turn the seventh graders into mush girls. The cafeteria cooks are trying to turn the Armenians into mushy Salisbury-steak eaters.

But Aram is in no way typical. Nothing mush about him. Agnes thinks about how the two of them combine in a totally original way. Their friendship is a little outpost way off down the road from the dumb, typical, annoying boy/girl mush world of Horace Mann.

Agnes starts to drift off. She sees Aram's eyes and the rare glimpse of a smile he left her with this afternoon. She sees him and his dog Razmig watching her on the benches from afar. The chilly wind is ruffling his hair. Agnes is blowing on her hands and Aram is still watching. For how long? Weeks?

"Ohmigosh!" She sits up, wide awake.

"Aram Keshishian is in love with me," Agnes whispers. "What in the world am I going to do?"

CHAPTER TWELVE

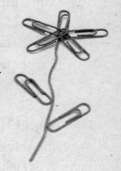

"Agnes," says Mrs. Parker, "I know you don't want me to comment about your clothes, but really . . ." She looks Agnes up and down. "Is your sweatshirt getting even baggier?"

"Mine's in the wash, and Dad never wears this," Agnes says. "It was a freebie. And wasn't it going to end up in the Salvation Army pile, anyway?"

"It's huge. I'm afraid you'll be sent home."

"People wear weirder things than this," Agnes says. If she had found a way to wear a sleeping bag to school, she would have. Anything to appear less of a love magnet to Aram Keshishian.

"Mom," Agnes says. "I have an enormous favor to ask you. I can't stay after school today. Is there any way you can pick me up?"

"Why can't you stay?"

"Because I need to come home. And do homework. Um, Internet-type homework. Which I can't do at school."

"I suppose I could come home a little early," Mrs. Parker says.

"Thank goodness," Agnes says.

She is still thinking up a lie about an important World History project when she sees Aram waiting by the school's front doors.

"Hello, Miss A!" he calls.

Agnes rarely sees him during the morning in natural light. Aram is always hiding in the art room or hanging out in a corner of the cafeteria with Edwin, spending as little time as possible out in the open.

"Hello!" he calls again, waving conspicuously.

This is worse than she imagined. "What are you doing out here?" Agnes asks.

"Nothing," Aram says. "I'm saying hello. Where is Prejean?"

"She came early this morning. She and Matthew are meeting with the teachers before school."

"Isn't it funny how that happened?" Aram says. "She loses the election and hates that guy, then sort of wins and likes him."

"I don't think she likes him all that much," Agnes insists.

"He likes Prejean," Aram says. "That's for sure. I

heard that in gym class." He nudges Agnes. "It's like there's something in the water here, right?"

"And what would that be?" Agnes asks stiffly.

Aram's eyes sparkle. "People are crushing on each other," he says.

Agnes slumps. "Uck," she says. Now there can be no doubt. She feels the same sense of emergency people do when something catches fire. She wants to stamp out the flame with a big pair of boots.

"Do you want me to carry something for you?" asks Aram, reaching toward her.

"No, no."

"Sure?"

"Let's walk," she says, hitching up her backpack. Aram tags along at her side.

"You are a fast walker," he says. "You take one step, I have to take two."

"Uh-huh."

"Maybe I need practice catching up. We could walk to class every morning. I could wait for you outside."

Agnes pretends not to hear.

As usual, the bell rings, Aram sits by Agnes, and Ms. Felson-Morales takes roll. "When you come over today," Aram says, "I have something to show you."

"I can't come over," Agnes says abruptly.

Aram looks disappointed. "Oh."

"Sorry, can't. Mom's picking me up. Homework."

Aram seems stumped. "You're going home early to do homework on a Friday?"

Agnes is getting irritated. "Yes, because I'm going to be too busy to do it the rest of the weekend."

"Then you'll come over on Monday maybe?"

"The thing is, Prejean isn't going to have track. So I won't be staying after for art room duty."

"But . . ."

"*Anymore,*" she adds sternly, just to make him stop asking questions.

"I see," Aram says softly.

Agnes senses his hurt and hates herself.

"Aram Keshishian?" says Ms. Felson-Morales.

"Here," says Aram. "Barely," he adds.

Part of Agnes wants to start over. Would it kill her to go to Aram's?

"Agnes Parker?" says Ms. Felson-Morales.

"Here," Agnes says, wishing she weren't.

Today, continuing their exploration of three-dimensional art, the class is to begin construction of papier-mâché masks. Ms. Felson-Morales passes around mounted pictures of tribal masks from Africa, Indonesia, and South America.

Agnes tries to change the direction of the morning. "This sounds good, eh, Aram?" She shows him a picture of an elephant mask with an extra-long trunk and tusks. "I like the idea of doing an animal."

"I don't know," Aram says. He shuffles through a few pictures, then stares at a mask that's a half-blue, half-red head with two noses and four eyes. "Something like this one I might do."

"Really?" Agnes says.

"It interests me," Aram says, unsmiling, "because it has two faces."

Agnes can't get him to say much more for the rest of the period. When class is over, he staggers off under the weight of his hastily-stuffed backpack without even saying good-bye.

I have one person who likes me. ONE, thinks Agnes. *And I treat him like dirt.*

Agnes hangs her head, enters the hall, and stumps past the wall of eighth-grade boys. She doesn't mind what they call out to her. She feels deserving of a little cruelty right now.

Prejean, meanwhile, is bubbling over. "Agnes, I've been waiting for you! You have got to come with me during morning break," she says. "It's official. The eighth-grade boys are going to get busted by the vice principal. I thought we could get a front-row seat."

"Who's busted?" asks Neidermeyer, coming seemingly from nowhere.

"The eighth-grade idiots," says Carmella.

"Aren't you glad?" Prejean asks Agnes. "Now you can stop dressing up like a . . ." Prejean flaps her arms.

"Like a Manta Ray?" says Carmella.

"Har! Is that what she is?" Neidermeyer says. "I was gonna say Caped Crusader."

Carmella guffaws.

"Thanks loads, Prejean," Agnes says. "Maybe you should save the front-row seats for Neidermeyer and Carmella." But she doesn't really mind Neidermeyer anymore. Her kind of taunting belongs to a time and place Agnes has outgrown.

All day Agnes looks around for Aram. At lunch, she sees Edwin eating by himself. What happened?

A drizzle descends on Horace Mann, sliming the pavement. When it's time to go home, Agnes stands with her hood pulled down over her eyes until she spots her mother's car. She runs over, finds the passenger side locked, and beats on the window.

"Boy," says Mrs. Parker. "You really want in, don't you?"

"Yes!" Agnes says. "I want home, and the weekend, and pajamas and TV."

Mrs. Parker doesn't ask why. She flips on the windshield wipers and turns up the heat. After a while, Agnes relaxes into the warmth and the *whomp-whomp* rhythm.

"Mom," Agnes says, "would you make me cinnamon toast?"

"Cinnamon toast sounds good," says Mrs. Parker.

"And cocoa? Please?"

Mrs. Parker agrees, but still leaves Agnes with her own thoughts all the way home.

"Brrrrr," says Agnes when she and her mother enter the house.

"How about you put a log in the fireplace?" Mrs. Parker suggests. "Your father picked up a box of them."

Scents of cinnamon and chocolate are filling the house by the time Agnes gets the fire started. Rain is now streaming down the living room windows. Mrs. Parker comes in with mugs and toast.

"On a tray? You are so nice," Agnes says. "This is like what a mom on TV would do."

"You're welcome," she says, setting the tray on the hearth. She takes her own mug of cocoa, sits, and opens a magazine.

It's weird. Agnes has been expecting her mom to start asking about the big homework assignment she had to rush home for. Or to pry about Agnes's horrible mood. Something!

"Mom?" Agnes says.

"Yes?"

"I love you."

Mrs. Parker looks up from her magazine and Agnes immediately knows what she's thinking: Agnes hasn't said "I love you" out loud in a very long time.

Why is that? Agnes wonders. But she's grateful when her mother simply says "Me too," and returns to her reading.

On Saturday, Agnes decides she must talk to Prejean. The girls go to Mr. Duval's garage workshop, choosing privacy over the thermostat.

"Do you remember when I was nice?" Agnes asks her friend.

"You're still nice," Prejean assures her.

"But even you said I'm grumpy," Agnes says.

"Yeah, you are grumpier," Prejean says frankly. "But I know you'd jump off a cliff for me, so I'm not complaining."

"So you're saying I'm loyal?"

"Exactly."

"Not anymore."

Prejean throws up her hands. "Is there something you want to talk about?"

Agnes blurts out the whole Aram story. "You were right way back when you said he was my fan. I didn't see it."

"That's also like you," Prejean says. "You're modest."

"So now are you going to spill everything to me about Matthew Blacker?" Agnes lifts a hammer from the work table. "Or do I need to threaten you?"

Prejean picks up a lug wrench. *"En garde,"* she says.

"No, really," Agnes says. "Do you like him?"

Prejean drops the wrench and sighs. "I realize he's a know-it-all. And bossy. He's a lot like me, actually. Except I think I have a better sense of humor."

"Then why, Prejean?"

"He's okay after you get to know him. I feel like, I don't know, I'm a good influence. Like, I'm training him to make jokes and be more fun."

"I get it. It's not a boy/girl thing. It's a training program." Agnes drums her fingers. "Hmmm. Do you think this is the result of your mom never allowing you to have any pets?"

Prejean shrugs. "Who knows what it is?"

"Aram already makes good jokes. But all I want is a good friend. We can't be a couple."

Prejean squints. "And I know why."

"Tell me."

"Because he's too short," Prejean says decisively.

"No way!" says Agnes.

"Maybe I'm wrong, but if he was normal size, don't you think you might not be so freaked out about him liking you?"

"I do not care about appearances. Look at me! Do I care?"

"You care about not *appearing* to care about appear-

141

ances. Or not appearing like you want people to see how you appear." Prejean stops, then laughs at herself. "What did I just say?"

Agnes laughs too. "Don't ask me."

But the question about Aram's size makes her think. Maybe that's what Aram, himself, believes. And there's no way to talk to him about it, really. She can't write a note saying, "Really. It's okay that you're short."

Agnes goes to art class on Monday determined to set things right. Aram isn't waiting for her out front, and he's not in class either. She sits and watches the door for his arrival.

He enters, late, and doesn't look her way. As a matter of fact, he sits at the front table on the other side of the room.

Agnes stares at the back of his head, willing him to turn around, but Aram is picking up none of her signals.

She is determined to get to him after class.

"Aram!" she calls. She has to say it twice.

He waits, his expression dark.

"Aram, I need to talk to you."

"I can't right now," he says. "But you can take this." He hands her an envelope.

"A note?"

"It's for your Cornell box," he says. "I'm going now."

142

"Wait!" Agnes says. But Aram won't.

The Cornell boxes are completed and locked in a display case by the front office. Agnes can't wait to see what this envelope is for. She backs up beside a bank of lockers and opens the letter.

DEAR MISS A,
I RESIGNED AS ART ROOM MANAGER. YOU
ARE IN CHARGE. CONGRATULATIONS
ON YOUR PROMOTION.
MR. A
EX-ART ROOM MANAGER

There's something else inside the envelope: a miniature replica of a plastic bottle, mounted on cardboard.

Gardenall WEED KILLER.

It takes a few moments to figure out the meaning. And then Agnes flashes on the afternoon he saved her art project, that hour of cutting out all those crazy daisies.

"He's killed our flowers!" Agnes says in disbelief.

And then silently she adds, *Or did I?*

CHAPTER THIRTEEN

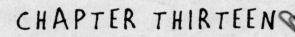

Agnes doesn't know Aram well enough to guess how long it takes him to get over hurt feelings. For days, he doesn't sit by her or look at her. Brian Olansky, of course, notices.

"Did you guys break up?" he asks sneakily, pretending to borrow glue.

"You can't break up with someone you aren't going with. He's just sitting somewhere else, that's all."

"Do you want me to ask him why?"

"No."

"Is it all right if I ask him?"

"Like I could stop you," says Agnes.

She knows Brian is an awful buttinsky, but she doesn't expect him to make a straight line for Aram right now—which he does.

Agnes wants to kill him. Why can't he get a life of

his own? She sees him straddling a chair, leaning into Aram, whispering. She expects Aram to wave Brian off, like the pest he is. But he talks back to him, instead.

What are they saying? she wonders. Aram gestures. Brian nods eagerly, as if to keep him talking.

When Brian goes back to his own chair, he keeps his back turned to her. Smugly, she thinks.

The whole scene makes her angry. How nasty was that "weed killer" thing, anyway? She tried to talk to Aram, and now he's confiding in Brian Olansky?

She cleans her hands of newspaper print and glue, and waits. When the bell rings, she watches Aram clamber off and then pounces on Brian before he can get away.

"What did he say?" Agnes demands. "I have a right to know and don't you dare leave out a word."

"He says he will never say a bad thing about you."

"Huh? What else?"

"I tried to get him to talk, but he won't tell me anything except that you're a great girl. That's it, period." Brian thinks hard. "Oh yeah, and he said it's none of my business."

"Well, it isn't," Agnes says. But she's secretly sorry Brian can't tell her more.

"By the way," says Brian. "Have you been in the library lately? All the eighth-grade guys are there now. It's the only place they're allowed to gang up, because

145

the principal put the halls off limits. It's really funny, because they can't talk there and they keep on driving the librarian insane."

Later, Agnes hears in gym how the librarian actually rolled up a newspaper and bopped Rex McNeeny on the head.

"Better she has to deal with it than us," Prejean says.

Pat Marie, the plump and shy girl, comes up and touches Prejean's shoulder. "I can't tell you. You've changed my life. Really. I used to wake up in the morning and instantly start dreading the halls."

"She should be *president*," Agnes says.

"But she's not," says Derry Timms. "And I have to say I told you so."

"No offense, Prejean," says Valerie.

"It's Geeky's fault!" hollers Neidermeyer. "Gutless," she whispers to Carmella.

"Hmmm. I wonder if *Neidermeyer* will be going to the dance," Valerie murmurs.

"Who all's going?" asks Derry. "Any of you guys?"

Pat Marie quickly shakes her head.

"I haven't decided," says Prejean. "It depends on whether I can get Agnes to come with me."

"I'll think about it," Agnes replies. Although she really doesn't want to.

Agnes doesn't dare approach Aram in class the next day. Brian will be straining to overhear everything. She sits back and listens to Ms. Felson-Morales talk about masks.

"Why do you suppose," the teacher asks, "people make and wear masks?"

"To rob banks?" says Brian.

"To conceal themselves, you mean? Yes," says Ms. Felson-Morales. "Any other reasons?"

"To scare people, like on Halloween," says another girl.

"To frighten people, yes," says the teacher. "How about those masks used for religious ceremonies? What might those masks be for?"

Agnes waits for someone to answer.

"That's a hard one, huh?" says Ms. Felson-Morales. "How about using a mask for transformation? To leave the old self behind?"

"Like Spider-Man?" says Brian.

"Sort of," says the teacher. "Not bad, actually, Brian."

Agnes looks down at her own mask, which she has been trying to make into a realistic face. It has eyeholes, cheekbones, a slit for a mouth. Does it say anything?

It reminds her of the face she tried to wear before she lost her "invisibility factor." She sees now that this mask needs something to deserve the viewer's interest: polka dots, a big nose, outrageous color.

Agnes smiles. How about a big sticking-out tongue? A mask that says: "So what?"

She brainstorms, thinking of materials she can use, when she sees Aram, bent over his own work. What kind of mask is he making?

The more Agnes wonders, the more she has to know. At last, she decides to hang out after class and find out for herself.

The bell rings. Agnes hangs back, pretending to have a question for Ms. Felson-Morales, as the kids stow their artwork on a newspaper-covered table. As soon as Aram is gone, she edges toward his mask and cranes her neck for a glimpse.

"You need something, Agnes?" asks her teacher.

"No, not really," she says. "I'm checking out the other kids' stuff. Curious."

"Aram's work is pretty interesting," says Ms. Felson-Morales.

Agnes feels funny, as if she's been caught in the act. "Is it?" she says. She looks around, making sure there's no one left from class, then bends over Aram's mask.

It's a fairly plain-looking face, not unlike the one Agnes started out with, only painted chalk white. But it has one distinguishing feature: a door in the forehead.

"It opens and closes," says Ms. Felson-Morales. "Try it."

Carefully, Agnes pulls at the door-like flap, which opens to a deep, built-in box. At the bottom is a single red blossom.

"A flower," Agnes says.

"Yes. It's simple. But it's compelling, don't you think?"

Agnes doesn't know what she expected; perhaps a little castle or one of those architectural things Aram likes to work on. The flower makes her feel hopeful somehow.

Aram opened that door for me once, she thinks. Why can't I get him to open it again?

It's the day before Thanksgiving break. Dance day. And Agnes is carrying not only her lunch, but a box decorated with wrapping paper. She's feeling in a holiday sort of mood, even though the wind is blowing the rain in gusts against the windshield.

"I'm going to be late today," she tells her mother. "I'm going to the dance at school."

"Well, good for you," says Mrs. Parker.

Prejean can't believe it. "What changed your mind?"

"For one thing," says Agnes, "I know how badly you want to go. As for the other reason—we'll see."

At lunch, Agnes moves past Prejean, Ashley, Derry, Valerie, and Natalie and boldly approaches Edwin and Aram.

"I brought a surprise," says Agnes. "Can I sit down?"

"I don't mind," says Edwin.

"It is a free cafeteria," Aram says.

Agnes places her wrapped box on the table and lifts the lid. "I made you the only American food I know how to make. Besides hot dogs."

"Cookies!" says Edwin.

"Chocolate chip," Agnes says. "To pay you back for the soup and dolmas. And I had a hard time coming up with something American that could match it."

Edwin reaches in, takes a cookie, and bites.

"Very good," he says, his mouth full.

"Thanks. They're definitely better than peanut butter sandwiches and American cheese."

Agnes hands a cookie to Aram. "Aren't you going to try one?"

He takes a nibble, then a bigger bite. "Okay, I give it to you. I of course have eaten this kind of cookie before, but these are good."

"The whole box is for you," Agnes says. "Share them with your family. They're my late thank-you."

"I am glad you didn't give us a box of American cheese," Aram says. "I have to be truthful."

Agnes laughs. "Or I could've brought a turkey."

Aram does not laugh back.

"Can I talk to you for a second?" Agnes asks.

Edwin grabs two cookies, then surrenders. "I'm going!" he says.

"I didn't just come over here for cookies," Agnes says. "I came to say . . ." She clears her throat. "I miss you."

"You change your mind too much," Aram says.

"I want to be friends. I always did. You are the best thing about this school."

Aram puts his elbows on the table. "That's not anything. You hate this school."

"I wouldn't hate it if you were my friend," Agnes says. "If you'd forgive me."

"I forgive," he says, but without warmth.

"Here's all I have to say: I know you. You are very much like me. You protect yourself. But with me, you didn't. And I stepped on you."

"No comment," Aram says.

"So I'm asking you to the dance today. I'll be there, waiting. Look for me. I'm sure you'll find me leaning against a wall."

"I don't dance," Aram says. "Not even for cookies. But thank you."

"I don't either," Agnes says. "But you can warm up the wall with me. I hope you come."

★ ★ ★

The gym has been decorated since this morning. Crepe paper and painted signs are slung above the bleachers. In gym, Mrs. Newton conducts calisthenics. "And please," she stresses, "avoid the DJ's table during exercise. Last spring, I had girls trying to high-jump the thing."

"They're hiring a DJ?" Agnes asks.

"That's why they call it a *dance*!" says Valerie.

After gym, Agnes dresses slowly. Prejean, all showered, combed, and gleamy, sits on the locker bench and waits.

Finally, as sounds of music echo from the gym, Agnes reluctantly crawls into her gigantic trademark sweatshirt and zips it to her chin. "I'm ready to party," she says.

Prejean shoots her a sympathetic look. "I know you don't want to do this," she says. "So thanks for being my buddy."

"Let's hurry before I change my mind," Agnes says.

The gym is darkened. A machine is whirling firefly lights around the walls. Most kids are clumped around the edges, watching. There are a few couples, and a group of eighth-grade girls dancing in a group. Shane McNeeny grabs a girl by the hand and drags her out on the floor.

"That's Ashley!" says Prejean.

"It is," says Agnes. "Poor girl."

Several more people get up their nerve after Shane leads the way. One of them is Matthew Blacker.

"Prejean," he says, tapping her on the shoulder. "Wanna dance?"

Prejean looks at Agnes questioningly.

"Go ahead," Agnes says, trying to sound nonchalant.

As she stands alone, scanning the crowd for someone to hang out with, Agnes can't help but note that Prejean, all elbows and knees, is an extraordinarily bad dancer. Agnes would feel horribly embarrassed for her if Prejean weren't laughing so hard herself. Matthew, concentrating intensely and shuffling as if he's in pain, is even worse.

Agnes hopes Prejean can't see Valerie and Derry standing on the sidelines whispering. The song goes on for what seems an eternity. As the music fades out, Agnes vows not to make sarcastic remarks when Prejean returns.

But Matthew asks for another dance!

They can't possibly be enjoying themselves, Agnes thinks. She waits through another song, and then another. Her mood sinks until she is sure she has made a serious mistake. It's no surprise that she's partnerless—didn't she tell Aram she'd be holding up the wall? But now she feels as if a spotlight is shining on her, announcing to the world what an isolated, weird, and difficult person she is.

"This is it," Agnes mutters. "This is the absolute last dance I ever go to."

Then she sees Aram at the other end of the gym.

The music booms as Aram swivels his head right and left. When he spots Agnes, he stops.

She raises her hand. He raises his back.

Never has she been so glad to see someone.

"You made it," Agnes says. "Oh, thank you. I am saved."

"Maybe you didn't think I was coming. Even I didn't know for sure until after school. And then I just had to do something first."

"What's that?"

Aram turns around in a circle. "See? No backpack. I put everything away in my locker."

"You're joining the locker people!" Agnes says. "Congratulations!"

"Yes," he says. "I am joining the locker people and the dancing people, all in one day."

"What made you change your mind?" Agnes asks.

"What made you ask me to the dance?" Aram asks back.

"Well," Agnes considers, "I've been being careful so far, you know? But being careful was making me very lonely."

"That's nothing," Aram says. "You should try being lonely and careful *and* carrying fifty pounds of back-pack. One of my shoulders is higher than the other. Maybe permanently."

The music softens and slides into a new song. It's a slow one, with the bass throbbing like a heartbeat. Aram looks up at Agnes. "You don't want to dance with me, do you?" he asks.

"What kind of question is that?" says Agnes. She realizes she's stalling. A slow song . . . What will people say?

But Aram is already standing with his arms out to take her. So she steps forward, gently, placing her hands on his shoulders. He leans in, and she rests her chin on the top of his head. They totter slowly. It isn't dancing as much as it feels that they're learning how to walk together.

Aram pulls away, holding Agnes at arm's length. "We must look ridiculous," he says.

"Think so?" Agnes says, pulling him back.

"Maybe I should stand on top of your shoes," he suggests. "Because if you haven't noticed, we have a dif-ference in height."

"Stay where you are," Agnes assures him. "This is actually sort of comfortable." She re-rests her chin upon his head and gazes into the dark.

Somewhere around the edges of the gym, there's

surely a Shane type laughing at the mismatched sight of them. And if Neidermeyer's watching? Agnes won't hear the end of it for weeks!

Agnes smiles. "Oh, so what?" she says out loud.

"Yes. So what?" echoes Aram Keshishian. And then, "Are you sure?"

"I'm positive," she says. And she means it.

So Aram is short. So Agnes is tall. So Prejean dances like a puppet. For now she'll leave it to the Derrys and Valeries—the mush people—to decide how impossible and embarrassing and bizarre everyone else is. Agnes Parker has already made up her mind: She's dancing this song to the very end, determined at last to keep an open heart.

About the Author

Kathleen O'Dell is the author of several children's novels, including *Agnes Parker . . . Girl in Progress*, which was a *Publishers Weekly* Flying Start winner; *Agnes Parker . . . Happy Camper?* and *Ophie Out of Oz*. She lives in Glendale, California, with her husband and two sons.